THE WHISPERING GAME

By

Aaron Shultz

The Whispering Game

Aaron Shultz

Published by Aaron Shultz, 2023.

THE WHISPERING GAME

First edition. December 1, 2023.

ISBN: 979-8223241324

Written by Aaron Shultz.

Table of Contents

CHAPTER 1

Emma Hartley stood in the hallway of Crestwood High School, her chestnut hair cascading down her back. Her deep-set blue eyes darted around, seeking out a mystery to unravel. She had an insatiable thirst for the unknown; it seemed like every question she answered led to another.

"Hey, Emma!" a classmate called from the crowd of students bustling around her. "Did you finish that math homework?"

"Of course," she replied, her eyes never ceasing their search. "I found a shortcut."

"Typical Emma," he laughed, shaking his head and walking away.

Crestwood High was a cacophony of sounds and colors: laughter echoed off the lockers, and the scent of lunchroom pizza wafted through the air. The students moved with purpose, each with their own mission as they navigated the crowded halls. It was a place of learning and growth, but unknown to many, it also held secrets waiting to be discovered.

"Miss Hartley," came a stern voice, cutting through the noise. Emma looked up to see Principal Eleanor Dawson standing in front of her, arms crossed. "Make sure you're not late for your next class."

"Of course, Principal Dawson," Emma said quickly, adjusting her backpack, feeling the weight of the woman's gaze even after she turned away.

"Man, she's intense," Emma muttered under her breath, watching as the principal stalked down the hall, her heels clicking on the linoleum floor. She knew that beneath Dawson's stern exterior lay a genuine concern for the students, but it was hard to remember that when faced with her intimidating presence.

As Emma continued down the hallway, she couldn't shake the feeling that something was amiss. Call it intuition or curiosity, but she had always been skilled at picking up on the subtle details others often overlooked. It was a skill that had served her well in the past, and now it was whispering that there was more to Crestwood High than met the eye.

"Focus, Emma," she told herself. "There's always something strange going on if you look hard enough." But even as she tried to dismiss her suspicions, her eyes continued their relentless search, scanning the faces of her classmates. And somewhere deep inside, she knew that the secrets of Crestwood High were just waiting to be unearthed.

Emma's eyes narrowed as she observed a group of students huddled together, their whispers barely audible above the steady hum of conversation. They exchanged furtive glances and secretive smiles, passing folded notes between them like contraband.

"Hey, Emma," greeted her friend, Lily McNees, snapping her out of her thoughts. Lily was small, with fiery red hair and a mischievous grin that hinted at her impulsive nature.

"Hey," Emma replied, her gaze still lingering on the whispering students. "You notice anything weird going on around here lately?"

"Like what?" chimed in another of Emma's friends, Daniel Roberts. Tall, lanky, and perpetually disheveled, Daniel was a walking encyclopedia of random knowledge - the kind of guy who could recite every element on the periodic table but couldn't remember where he'd left his keys.

"Like... I don't know," Emma said hesitantly, feeling foolish for even bringing it up. "People acting secretive, passing notes, whispering..."

"Sounds like The Whispering Game," Lily murmured, her green eyes alight with curiosity. "I've heard a few people talking about it."

"Wait, The Whispering Game?" Daniel asked, raising an eyebrow. "What's that?"

"Nobody knows for sure," Lily admitted, her voice dropping to a conspiratorial whisper. "Some sort of secret club or game. There are challenges you have to complete, and if you succeed, you get... something."

"Something?" Emma echoed skeptically. "That's pretty vague."

"Isn't that the point?" Daniel mused, his brown eyes twinkling with amusement. "It's supposed to be mysterious, right? That's what makes it so intriguing."

"Maybe," Emma conceded, her interest piqued despite herself. Her mind raced with questions: who had started this game, and why? What were the challenges like, and what happened to those who failed them? And most importantly, how could she resist the urge to uncover the truth?

"Let's keep an eye on it," she suggested, her voice firm with resolve. "If something's going on, we'll find out."

"Deal," Lily agreed, her grin growing wider. "This is going to be fun."

"Fun?" Daniel snorted. "You have a weird idea of fun, Lily."

"Hey, you're friends with us," she retorted, poking him in the chest. "What does that say about you?"

"Good point," he conceded, rubbing the spot where she'd jabbed him. "I guess I'm just as weird as you are."

As the trio continued down the hall, Emma's thoughts swirled around The Whispering Game - and she couldn't shake the feeling that they were about to stumble into something far more dangerous than they could possibly imagine.

The bell rang, signaling the end of fourth period. As Emma walked through the crowded hallway, she couldn't help but notice the animated chatter and hushed whispers among her fellow students. Her deep-set blue eyes darted around, trying to discern any snippets of information about The Whispering Game.

"Did you hear? Jason completed his third challenge last night," a girl whispered excitedly to her friend, just as Emma passed by their lockers.

"Really?" the other girl replied, her eyes wide with curiosity. "What was it?"

"Something about finding a hidden message in the school library after hours," she confided, lowering her voice even further.

Emma's heart raced at the thought of secret messages hidden within Crestwood High School, fueling her desire to know more. She made a mental note to visit the library during her lunch break, hoping to find any clues that might lead her closer to understanding the game.

As the days went by, Emma dedicated every free moment she had to investigating The Whispering Game. Between classes, she would covertly observe her classmates, looking for any signs they were involved in the game. During lunch breaks, she scoured the school grounds and the library, searching for anything out of the ordinary.

"Hey, Em," Lily said one day, catching up to her in the hallway. "You've been acting pretty distant lately. Everything okay?"

"Yeah, I'm fine," Emma replied unconvincingly, forcing a smile. "Just have a lot on my mind, I guess."

Lily raised an eyebrow, clearly not buying Emma's explanation, but she didn't push further. Instead, she patted her friend on the shoulder and walked away, leaving Emma alone with her thoughts.

Deep down, Emma knew she should share her investigation with her friends and involve them in her pursuit of the truth. But she also feared putting them in danger, knowing that the game was becoming more popular and, seemingly, more dangerous. She wrestled with her decision, torn between loyalty to her friends and her burning curiosity.

"Emma Hartley," a voice whispered behind her during a free period. Startled, she turned around to find a folded piece of paper on the floor. It bore her name, written in a hurried scrawl. Her heart pounding, she picked it up and unfolded it, revealing her first cryptic task from The Whispering Game.

"Find the key hidden in shadows where knowledge lives."

Emma read the message several times, her mind racing. She knew now that there would be no turning back - she was in the game, whether she liked it or not. And she couldn't help but wonder what consequences awaited her as she delved deeper into The Whispering Game's mysteries.

"Hey, Emma!" called out Max from across the bustling school cafeteria. His dark hair was messy, and his eyes gleamed with excitement. "You won't believe what just happened."

Emma looked up from her book, her deep-set blue eyes narrowing in curiosity. "What's up?" she asked, sliding into a chair next to him.

"Okay," Max began, his voice hushed as he leaned in closer. "So, I got this message today." He pulled out a crumpled piece of paper from his pocket, smoothing it out on the table. "It said: 'Find the faceless portrait in the room of creativity.'"

"Faceless portrait?" Emma echoed, her curiosity piqued even more.

"Yeah," chimed in Sarah, who had been listening from the next table. She nervously twisted a strand of her blonde hair around her finger. "And when I found it, there was another clue hidden behind it. It led me to a secret door in the art room. Crazy, right?"

"Secret door?" Emma muttered, her mind racing with possibilities. The game was twisting its way through their school, leaving riddles and enigmas in its wake.

"Attention, students!" Principal Dawson's stern voice boomed over the intercom, cutting through the lively chatter. "I've been informed that some of you have been engaging in disruptive behavior during school hours. This must cease immediately. Anyone found participating in such activities will face severe consequences. Remember, you're here to learn and grow, not to waste time on foolish games."

Emma exchanged looks with her friends, knowing that Principal Dawson referred to The Whispering Game. Her concern for her friends' safety gnawed at her, but her inner conflict remained unresolved - should she join them or stay on the sidelines?

"Hey, Em," whispered Max, bringing her back to the present moment. "Have you gotten any messages?"

Emma hesitated, recalling the cryptic task she had received earlier. She wasn't sure if she should share it with them or keep it to herself. Her eyes darted around the cafeteria, searching for any sign of eavesdroppers.

"Emma?" Sarah prompted, her green eyes filled with concern.

"Um, yeah," she admitted finally, her voice barely audible. "I got one today."

"Really?" Max exclaimed, his curiosity now directed at her. "What's your challenge?"

"Find the key hidden in shadows where knowledge lives," Emma recited from memory.

"Ooh, that sounds interesting," said Sarah, her eyes wide with intrigue.

"Be careful, Emma," warned Max, his expression serious. "We don't know what we're getting ourselves into."

"Neither do I," Emma thought, swallowing hard as her gaze drifted back to the crumpled clue on the table. The game was pulling her deeper, and there was no telling where it would lead.

Emma's heart raced as she roamed the crowded hallways of Crestwood High, her deep-set blue eyes scanning the faces around her. The Whispering Game had cast a dark shadow over the school; its sinister presence was palpable in every corner. She could feel its grip tightening on her friends, and it seemed to be spreading like a contagious disease among the students.

"Hey, did you hear about Maria?" whispered one girl to another as they passed by, their voices barely audible above the hum of conversation. "She got a challenge last night."

"Really?" replied the other, eyes wide with disbelief. "What was it?"

"Can't tell," the first girl smirked, tapping the side of her nose conspiratorially. "It's a secret."

Emma watched them walk away, her stomach twisting with unease. It wasn't just her friends who were getting sucked into the game anymore. Now, it seemed that everyone was playing.

"Em!" Sarah called out, approaching with Max in tow. Her red hair bounced as she walked, and her green eyes sparkled with excitement. "You won't believe the challenge I got this morning!"

"Another one?" Emma sighed, trying to mask her growing concern. "Sarah, we have to be careful. This is getting dangerous."

"Relax, Em," Max chimed in, his dark, curly hair falling over his forehead. "We're smart enough to know when to quit, right?"

"Are we, though?" Emma thought, biting her lip as she looked from Max to Sarah. They were both so bright, so full of potential. Why were they risking everything for a stupid game?

"Besides," Sarah added, grinning mischievously. "You're in it now too, aren't you? How's your challenge going, by the way?"

"Slowly," Emma admitted, glancing down at her feet. The truth was, she hadn't made any progress at all. The key hidden in shadows where knowledge lived - what did that even mean? "We need to stick together on this," she said, looking up at her friends. "Promise me you'll be careful."

"Of course," Sarah agreed, nodding solemnly. "Safety first."

"Always, Em," Max reassured her, his brown eyes warm and unwavering.

But as they walked away, leaving Emma alone in the hallway, she couldn't shake the feeling that something terrible was about to happen. What if one of them got hurt? What if the challenges became too much for them to handle?

"Find the key hidden in shadows where knowledge lives," Emma muttered under her breath, determined to solve her own challenge before it consumed her. She would do whatever it took to keep her friends safe, even if it meant diving headfirst into the dangerous world of The Whispering Game herself.

Emma's heart raced as she observed from a distance the growing number of students huddled in corners, exchanging whispers and furtive glances. She bit her lip, her deep-set blue eyes darting back and forth, trying to take in every detail.

"Join us, Em," Max had said, his voice filled with an unsettling excitement. "It's just a game."

But was it really? Her gut told her otherwise. The challenges were becoming more cryptic, the stakes higher. Emma shuddered at the thought of what might happen if things went too far.

"Hey, Emma!" Sarah called out, snapping her out of her thoughts.

"Hey." Emma forced a smile, her mind still consumed by the game's potential dangers.

"Did you hear about the latest challenge?" Sarah asked, her eyes wide with curiosity.

Emma hesitated, torn between wanting to protect her friends and the burning desire to know more. "No," she finally admitted. "What is it?"

"Find the truth hidden within the lie," Sarah whispered, a grin spreading across her face. "Exciting, huh?"

"Sure," Emma replied, her stomach twisting in knots. She needed to make a choice: stay on the sidelines or dive into the mystery headfirst.

"Emma, are you okay?" Sarah's concern was evident in her voice.

"Fine," she lied, her chest tightening. "I'm just... thinking."

"About the game?" Sarah studied her friend closely.

"Yeah," Emma murmured, her resolve wavering. Was it worth risking her safety, her sanity, for this twisted game?

"Listen," Sarah said softly. "Whatever you choose, we'll support you. But I think you'd be great at it."

"Thanks," Emma whispered, her mind made up. She would join the game - not for the thrill, but to watch over her friends and save them from themselves if necessary.

"Let's go find Max," Sarah suggested, linking arms with Emma and leading her down the hall. "He'll be thrilled you're in."

But just as they rounded a corner, a folded note slipped from Emma's locker, fluttering to the ground. She picked it up hesitantly, her heart pounding in her chest.

"Welcome to The Whispering Game," it read. "Your first challenge: Unmask the liar hiding amongst your closest allies."

Emma's breath caught in her throat. She glanced at Sarah, her eyes narrowed with suspicion. What had she gotten herself into?

CHAPTER 2

As Emma stood in the dimly lit hallway, her heart pounding with anticipation, she hesitated for a moment. Her deep-set blue eyes scanned the mysterious letter that had arrived earlier that day, beckoning her to participate in "The Whispering Game." A sense of excitement coursed through her veins, driving her curiosity and sense of adventure. She knew there was no turning back now.

"Alright," she whispered to herself, determination etched across her face. "Let's play this game."

Moments later, Emma received her first cryptic task via text message. The words on the screen seemed to dance before her eyes, offering a challenge that she could not resist: "Seek the emerald eye hidden in darkness, where no shadows fall, yet light still hides."

Emma furrowed her brow, trying to decipher the meaning behind the puzzling clue. Emerald eye? Darkness? Shadows? Her mind raced with possibilities, each more intriguing than the last. She read the message again, searching for any hidden meaning or pattern.

"Okay, Emma," she muttered under her breath, rolling up her sleeves as she prepared to dive headfirst into the unknown. "You've always loved a good mystery. Let's see what you've got."

With her heart racing and her curiosity piqued, Emma couldn't help but feel a thrill at the prospect of participating in the game. Little did she know that her decision would set into motion a series of events that would change her life forever.

"Emerald eye, darkness, shadows, light," Emma whispered to herself as she walked briskly through the school halls. Her eyes scanned her surroundings, searching for anything that could help her unlock the riddle.

"Hey, Emma!" a familiar voice called out, but she barely acknowledged it, too focused on her task.

"Sorry, got to go!" she replied hurriedly, determined not to be distracted by anyone or anything.

As she considered the cryptic message, her thoughts turned to the library – a place often filled with shadows and hidden corners. She knew that's where she'd find her answer, or at least a starting point.

"Where no shadows fall, yet light still hides," she repeated, pushing open the heavy library doors. The dimly lit room was a labyrinth of bookcases and tables, with students scattered throughout. It was a place where knowledge thrived in the shadows, and Emma's intuition told her that this was the key to solving the riddle.

"Let's see..." she muttered, absently biting her lip. Methodically, she moved from one aisle to another, her fingertips brushing against the spines of countless books. The scent of old paper and ink hung in the air, mixing with the faint hum of whispers and rustling pages.

"Come on, think, Emma," she urged herself, feeling the pressure build within her chest. She knew there must be some connection between the emerald eye and the absence of shadows. And then it hit her – the stained glass window in the back of the library.

"Of course!" she exclaimed, her eyes widening in realization. The window depicted an intricate scene of a dragon guarding a treasure hoard. At its center was a large, green gemstone – the emerald eye.

With a newfound purpose, Emma made her way toward the window. Her heart pounded in her ears, each step bringing her closer to the answer. She could feel the tension in the air, thick and palpable. But she refused to let herself be intimidated by the unknown.

"Alright," she murmured, standing in front of the window. It cast a kaleidoscope of colors across the floor, shadows dancing around her feet. But there was one spot untouched by the light – a small alcove hidden behind a bookcase.

"Where no shadows fall, yet light still hides," she whispered, her pulse quickening. Tentatively, she reached out and pulled the bookcase aside, revealing a dusty, long-forgotten space.

"Okay, Emma... this is it," she thought, swallowing hard. Little did she know that by delving deeper into the game, she was inching closer to the malevolent force lurking just beyond her grasp.

Emma stepped into the alcove, her heart racing. She reached out and felt something cold and smooth. Prying it from the wall, she discovered a small, ornate key. It glinted in the dim light, beckoning her to continue. Near the hidden key Emma located an old journal and several new clippings shoved between the pages.

"Task completed," she whispered triumphantly, her eyes sparkling with excitement. The thrill of solving the puzzle and uncovering the hidden treasure sent a shiver down her spine. Emma couldn't help but feel a sense of accomplishment, despite the lingering unease about the game's true intentions.

"Hey, Emma!" called a voice from behind her. Startled, she quickly hid the key and journal in her pocket and turned to face Lucas Finch, his sandy hair disheveled as he approached her, grinning. "I saw you slip back here. What are you up to?"

"Nothing, just... exploring," she lied, trying to sound casual. But Lucas's keen intuition picked up on her evasiveness, curiosity piqued.

"Exploring, huh?" he said, raising an eyebrow. "You wouldn't happen to be playing that new game everyone's talking about, would you? The Whispering Game?"

"Maybe," Emma admitted, her cheeks reddening. "I just finished my first task."

"Interesting," mused Lucas, scratching his chin. "Ava and I have been hearing about this game too. We're thinking about giving it a try."

"Really?" Emma asked, surprised by their interest. "Well, it's definitely challenging, if that's what you're looking for."

"Challenging is good," Ava Martinez chimed in, appearing beside Lucas. Her curly black hair framed her sharp brown eyes that seemed to pierce right through Emma. "I'm always up for a good puzzle. Plus, I've got some mad hacking skills that might come in handy."

"Alright then," Emma said, hesitating for a moment before deciding that she could trust them. "Maybe we can work together on this."

"Sounds like a plan," Lucas agreed with a grin, while Ava nodded in approval.

"Who knows what we'll uncover?" Emma mused, her blue eyes reflecting the anticipation and excitement of the unknown. As they walked away from the hidden alcove, the three of them couldn't help but feel drawn deeper into the mysteries of The Whispering Game, unaware of the darkness lurking just beneath the surface.

The following day at school, Emma couldn't help but notice the growing buzz around The Whispering Game. It seemed that everywhere she looked, clusters of students were huddled together, whispering excitedly and poring over cryptic notes. Lucas and Ava, who had officially decided to take part in the game, were no exception.

"Look at this," Ava said, unfolding a crumpled piece of paper and placing it on the cafeteria table. Her eyes were alight with curiosity as she traced her finger over the intricate pattern drawn on it. "It's my first task. I have no idea what it means, but I'm dying to find out."

"Same here," agreed Lucas, showing them his own note. The words were written backward, forcing him to hold it up to a mirror just to read it. "I've never seen anything like this before. It's like someone went to great lengths to create these clues."

Emma nodded, feeling a thrill run down her spine. They were all in this together now, bound by their shared sense of adventure and desire to solve the enigma that was The Whispering Game. She watched as Lucas and Ava exchanged ideas and suggestions, their voices low and animated.

"Hey, maybe we can use your hacking skills to dig up more information about this game," Lucas suggested to Ava. "See if there are any patterns or common threads among the players."

"Good idea," Ava replied, tapping her fingers on the table thoughtfully. "But we need to be careful. We don't want to get caught."

"Definitely," Emma chimed in, her heart pounding with anticipation. "We should also keep track of our progress and share our findings with each other. Who knows what we might uncover?"

"Agreed," Lucas said, locking eyes with both Emma and Ava. "Whatever this game is, we're going to figure it out together."

As the trio delved deeper into their tasks, they began to notice more and more of their classmates getting involved in The Whispering Game. Some were drawn by the challenge of solving riddles and puzzles, while others were motivated by a desire for excitement and novelty. The game was spreading like wildfire, its allure impossible to resist.

But amidst the exhilaration and camaraderie, Emma couldn't shake the nagging feeling that something was off. What was the purpose behind this game? And who was orchestrating it all? She knew she had to find out, even if it meant putting herself in danger.

"Guys," she whispered urgently to Lucas and Ava, "we need to be prepared for anything. This game might be more than we bargained for."

"Then we'll face it together," Lucas replied firmly, his eyes full of resolve.

"Whatever it takes," added Ava, her voice unwavering.

And with that, the three of them plunged headfirst into the unknown, determined to unravel the mysteries of The Whispering Game and confront whatever darkness lay ahead.

The school bell echoed through the empty hallways as Emma hurriedly stuffed her books into her bag. She glanced around, taking in the hushed conversations and furtive glances that filled the air like static electricity.

"Did you hear about Sam?" whispered a girl to her friend, eyes wide with excitement. "He completed the third task last night."

"Really?" her friend gasped. "What was it?"

"I don't know," the first girl admitted. "But everyone's talking about it."

Emma couldn't help but feel a chill down her spine. The Whispering Game had become more than just a pastime; it was an obsession, seeping into every corner of the school like a slow-acting poison.

"Hey, Emma," Ava greeted her with a conspiratorial smile as she approached Lucas and Emma by their lockers. "I've been hearing whispers all day. Seems like everyone's trying to outdo each other."

"Seems so," Emma replied, unable to mask her unease. "It's like the whole school's under a spell."

"Speaking of which," Lucas interjected, his eyes narrowing as he leaned in closer. "Have you guys made any progress on your tasks?"

Ava shook her head, frustration evident on her face. "Not yet, but I'm close. I can feel it."

"Me neither," Emma admitted, her thoughts racing. She wondered if the others were experiencing the same sense of foreboding that she felt creeping up on her, or if they were simply too enthralled by the game to notice.

"Listen," she said urgently, lowering her voice. "We need to stay sharp. Something about this game doesn't sit right with me."

"Agreed," Lucas said, his voice equally hushed. "We'll keep our eyes peeled and make sure we're not getting in over our heads."

"Definitely," Ava chimed in, her expression serious. "We'll solve this mystery, whatever it takes."

As Emma nodded in agreement, she couldn't shake the feeling that they were on the cusp of something much larger than any of them could comprehend. The mysteries of The Whispering Game seemed to grow deeper and darker with each passing day, and as the game tightened its grip on the school, she knew that they would have to confront its secrets sooner rather than later.

"Be careful, you two," she whispered, her voice barely audible above the din of the hallway. And with a final nod, the trio dispersed, their resolve steeled by the knowledge that they were navigating treacherous waters.

But even as they focused on the tasks ahead, the shadow of The Whispering Game loomed over them, a silent presence that threatened to consume them all. And though they couldn't have known it then, their journey into the heart of darkness had only just begun.

CHAPTER 3

Emma paced back and forth in her bedroom, her chestnut hair swaying with each step. The dim light from her desk lamp cast eerie shadows on the walls, doing little to calm her racing thoughts. She bit her lip, deep-set blue eyes reflecting the conflict within. Should she continue playing The Whispering Game? Or was it time to walk away?

Shadows danced on the walls as Emma rifled through her collection of old books, maps, and newspaper clippings she gathered from the school library. Chilled air crept under the door, whispering secrets only she could hear. Emma placed the found key and old journal on her wooden desk.

"Think," she muttered. "Where does this key and journal lead me next?"

"Emma?" A voice called from the hallway, her mother. "Lights out in five minutes!"

"Okay, Mom!" She replied quickly, heart racing. Time was slipping away, and she had yet to unearth a single clue.

Her eyes scanned the pile of information, desperately searching for something - anything - that would lead her closer to finding the next clue. Then, she saw it: a cryptic message, hidden among the yellowed pages of the old journal.

"Th3 W1nd Wh15p3r5" was scribbled in a barely legible script. Numbers replacing letters - a simple code, but one that took her a moment to decipher. "The Wind Whispers" she whispered, eyebrows furrowing.

"Time's up!" Her mom called again, footsteps approaching.

"Coming!" Emma hurriedly concealed her research under the floorboards, plunging the room into darkness just as her mother opened the door. The secret remained safe, for now.

Sleep eluded her that night. Vague shapes formed in the darkness, taunting her with their elusive meaning. Emma rolled over, mind buzzing with thoughts of codes and cyphers.

"Wind whispers... what does that mean?" she pondered, frustration mounting. "Could it be... No, that's too simple."

"Or is it?" she challenged herself, considering the possibility. If the clue was about wind, perhaps it was pointing her toward a specific location - somewhere windy, like a coastal town or a valley between mountains.

"Alright, let's think," she whispered into the night. "If I cross-reference this with the map" - her fingers traced imaginary lines in the air - "it might lead me to... there!"

"Where?" she asked herself, heart pounding. "I can't do this in the dark."

"Tomorrow," she decided, determination burning within her. "Tomorrow, I'll find the next clue."

"Sleep now, Emma" she coaxed herself, her breath slowing as her mind finally allowed her a reprieve from the puzzle.

The morning light brought clarity, and with it, a renewed sense of purpose. As soon as she could, Emma retrieved her hidden research, her fingers deftly tracing the lines on the map, connecting dots only she could see.

"Got it!" she exclaimed under her breath, a triumphant smile crossing her face. The coordinates led her to a small coastal village, notorious for its strong winds and rocky cliffs.

"Perfect," she thought, her mind racing with possibilities. "I'll start my search there."

Emma knew that each step she took brought her closer to unraveling the mystery of The Whispering Game. And she refused to back down until every last secret was laid bare.

"Hey, Emma!" a voice called out as she approached the school gate. She recognized it instantly - it was Zack, one of her classmates who was also playing The Whispering Game.

"Hey," she replied cautiously, her heart pounding with both dread and anticipation. Would he have any new information?

"Listen," Zack said, leaning in closer, his voice barely audible. "I know we're not supposed to talk about the game, but I think something's off. People are getting hurt."

"Really?" Emma's eyes widened with concern. "People have been getting in accidents trying to find these clues and solve these puzzles, people are obsessed." The game was becoming more dangerous than she had initially thought. She couldn't help but feel responsible for the other players; after all, they were just kids like her, drawn into this twisted mystery.

"Emma," Zack continued, urgency in his voice. "You've got to do something. You're the smartest person I know. If anyone can figure this out, it's you."

Emma hesitated, her mind racing through possible scenarios and consequences. She knew that continuing her investigation could put her at risk, but the thought of her friend's suffering compelled her to act.

"Alright," she whispered, determination setting in. "But we need to keep this quiet. I don't want anyone else getting involved."

"Understood." Zack nodded solemnly, relief flickering across his face.

"I can't do this alone Zack, I need your help." Emma stated. "I think I know where the next clue is leading me, but I need a partner to travel with me." Zack nodded, "you can always count on me, Emma."

That afternoon, Emma and Zack found themselves in the small coastal village, only a few short miles from her home. They were careful not to draw attention, aware that someone might be watching their every move. "What am I even looking for?" thought Emma.

"Okay, think," she muttered under her breath, scanning the area for anything unusual. "What am I missing?"

As Emma and Zack delved deeper into the mystery, each step brought new challenges and unsettling revelations. And yet, she refused to give up, driven by her desire to protect her friends from the game's malevolent grasp.

Walking along the shoreline, the afternoon warmth drew to a close and the cool air began to roll off the ocean. Shivers race up and now Emma's spine while her mind scrambles.

"Come on, Emma, think," she whispered to herself, her breath visible in the cold air. Just then her eyes catch what she's been looking for, a long-forgotten cemetery loomed off the side of the road. The decayed iron and steel sign reads, "Whisper Cemetery."

Emma and Zack were standing at the edge of an abandoned graveyard, the moon casting eerie shadows through the towering trees that surrounded it. The sound of rustling leaves, carried by the wind, sent shivers down Emma's spine.

The silent night air was cut short by a loud yell, "Hey, I found something!" yelled Zack. He held up a rusty key, excitement dancing in his eyes.

"Good job," Emma said, her determination fueling her despite the mounting obstacles. "We're getting closer."

"Are you sure about this, Emma?" Zack asked, concern etched on his face. "It feels like we're way out of our depth here."

"I know, but we can't stop now," she replied, her voice unwavering. Her deep-set blue eyes searched the graveyard, trying to find a connection between the key and their surroundings. "People are counting on us."

"Alright then," he conceded, handing her the key. "Lead the way."

As they ventured further into the graveyard, the ground beneath them grew increasingly uneven, the gnarled roots of ancient trees reaching out like grasping hands. Emma's chestnut hair whipped around her face as another gust of wind swept through the area, making her shudder involuntarily.

"Look!" Emma pointed towards a crypt hidden among the overgrown foliage, its wrought iron gate twisted and rusted. "The key might fit there."

"Let's hope so," Zack muttered, following her as they approached the crypt. As Emma inserted the key into the lock, the gate creaked open, revealing a dark passage leading underground.

"Here goes nothing," she thought, taking a deep breath before stepping into the darkness. The musty smell of decay filled her nostrils as she descended the narrow stone steps, the only sound the echo of their footsteps and the pounding of her heart.

"Emma," Zack whispered, his voice trembling. "What if we're not alone down here?"

"Stay close," Emma instructed, her eyes scanning the darkness for any sign of danger. "And be ready for anything."

As they continued deeper into the crypt, the air grew colder, the dank walls pressing in on them. Suddenly, a faint scratching noise reached Emma's ears, making her freeze in her tracks.

"Did you hear that?" She asked, her pulse racing.

"Y-yeah," Zack stammered, his face pale under the dim light of their flashlight.

"Let's keep going," Emma insisted, her determination unwavering despite her fear. "We can't turn back now."

With every step, the scratching grew louder, the oppressive atmosphere intensifying. As they rounded a corner, they were met with a sight that made their blood run cold: a wall covered in cryptic symbols, fresh scratches still visible.

"Wh-what is this?" Zack stuttered, his voice barely audible.

"Another clue," Emma said, her mind racing to decipher the meaning of the symbols. "And a warning."

They stood there, surrounded by darkness and mystery, their breaths coming in short gasps. Yet, even in the face of such chilling revelations, Emma's resolve remained unshakable. She would uncover the truth behind the Whispering Game, no matter what it took.

"Zack, we need to press on," Emma said, her voice firm and resolute. She could feel the weight of her decision bearing down on her, but she refused to let it hinder her progress.

"Alright," Zack replied, a hint of trepidation in his voice. He followed closely behind her as they ventured further into the unknown.

The air grew even colder, and an eerie silence enveloped them. The only sound to be heard was their own breaths, which seemed deafening in the all-consuming quiet. Their flashlight flickered ominously, casting distorted shadows on the ancient walls.

"Emma, are you sure about this?" Zack asked, his anxiety palpable.

"Positive." Her response was immediate, her conviction unwavering. "We have to know the truth."

As they moved forward, the darkness seemed to slither around them like a living entity, wrapping its tendrils around their limbs and threatening to drag them under. Emma's heart pounded in her chest, a steady drumbeat urged her to keep going.

"Wait," she whispered, her hand reaching out to stop Zack. "Look at this."

"More symbols?" he inquired, peering over her shoulder.

"No... something else. A map, maybe?" Emma studied the intricate lines etched into the stone, her brow furrowed in concentration.

"Could be," Zack agreed hesitantly. "But where does it lead?"

"Only one way to find out." With renewed determination, Emma traced her finger along the path indicated by the map, her eyes alight with curiosity.

"Are we really doing this?" Zack asked, his voice wavering ever so slightly.

"Absolutely," Emma replied, her tone laced with steel. "We've come too far to turn back now."

"Okay, then," Zack sighed. "Lead the way."

With each step, the oppressive darkness seemed to loosen its grip on them. The air grew warmer, the silence less suffocating. Though fear still gnawed at the edges of her mind, Emma's resolve only strengthened.

"Whatever happens," she thought, "I won't back down."

As they reached the end of the tunnel, a faint light beckoned them forward. With one final glance at Zack, Emma took a deep breath and stepped into the unknown, her decision irrevocable. There was no turning back now.

Finally reaching the end of the tunnel, a shiny object on the ground catches their eyes. Reaching down to the cement floor, Emma picks up what she soon realizes is a large kitchen knife. "Zack, does this look like blood on the blade of this knife?" Emma's shaky voice whispers. Emma quickly drops the knife to the ground making a loud metallic sound that echoes down the tunnel.

"Let's get out of here Emma, something tells me we are in over our heads."

CHAPTER 4

The black sedan gleamed in the sunlight near Crestwood's town center, catching Emma's attention. Leaning against it was a man with cropped gray hair and a stern expression, setting him apart from the townspeople in the square.

Detective Thompson, she murmured to herself, observing as he surveyed the area with the practiced eye of an investigator. His presence intrigued her, prompting questions about what could have brought him to Crestwood.

As Emma thought about the recent peculiar events in Crestwood and the unsettling discovery of a bloody knife in the tunnel, her heart raced. The persistent rumors of "The Whispering Game" fueled her determination to unravel the mystery. Now, with Detective Riley Thompson on the scene, she sensed that the puzzle pieces were falling into place.

"Emma?" Sarah, her friend, interrupted, pulling at her arm. "What are you staring at?"

"Nothing, I just... I need to go talk to someone." Emma shook off Sarah's grip and navigated through the crowd toward the detective. Her mind raced, formulating the right questions and the perfect approach.

As the sun dipped lower, casting long shadows across the bustling town square, Emma's heart raced. She approached Detective Thompson, who stood with his arms folded, observing the passing crowds.

"Detective Thompson?" Her voice faltered slightly as she introduced herself. "I'm Emma Hartley."

"Miss Hartley." He nodded curtly, studying her with a hint of curiosity. "What can I do for you?"

"I wanted to talk about..." She hesitated, glancing around to ensure no one was listening. "The investigation."

"Which one?" His gaze remained cool, and Emma felt a sudden surge of determination.

"The Whispering Game," she said firmly, locking eyes with him.

"Ah." A flicker of surprise passed over his face before he quickly composed himself. "That's just some teenage nonsense, isn't it?"

"Please," Emma implored, her hands trembling. "I think there's more to it than that. There have been... incidents."

"Look, Miss Hartley," he sighed, rubbing his temple. "I've seen a lot of strange things in my time, but this game seems like nothing more than a rumor. Kids playing pranks on each other."

"Detective," Emma pressed on, desperation creeping into her voice. "People are getting hurt. And I think whoever's behind it is dangerous."

He eyed her carefully, weighing her words. Finally, he nodded slowly. "Alright. Let's find somewhere quieter to talk."

As they walked through the crowded streets, Emma caught sight of Principal Eleanor Dawson, talking animatedly to a group of parents. She shuddered involuntarily, remembering the stern woman's warnings about The Whispering Game.

"Thank you," Emma whispered to Detective Thompson as they found an empty bench in a secluded corner. "I know it's hard to believe, but I'm sure there's something sinister going on."

"Alright," he said, leaning back and folding his arms. "Tell me everything you know about this game."

Emma took a deep breath and began to recount the strange happenings she had witnessed. As Detective Thompson listened intently, his skepticism slowly giving way to concern, she felt a glimmer of hope that together they might uncover the truth behind The Whispering Game.

"Last week," Emma began, her voice low and steady, "I found a note on my locker. It was written in crimson ink and said, 'You're invited to play The Whispering Game.'"

She pulled out the crumpled paper from her backpack, handing it to Detective Thompson.

"Looks like a prank," he muttered, examining the note for a moment before returning his gaze to Emma.

"Except, since then," she continued, "I've seen strange things. People whispering secrets in hushed tones, passing along cryptic messages. One girl, Sarah, got so scared she locked herself in the bathroom for hours."

Emma paused, recalling the terror in Sarah's eyes when they finally managed to coax her out. She knew she had to make Thompson understand just how serious this game was.

"Then there's Danny," she went on. "He played the game and ended up in the hospital, because of some secret he couldn't handle. His parents think it was an accident, but I know better."

Detective Thompson furrowed his brow, now giving Emma his full attention.

"Both incidents happened after the game started circulating around school," she added. "And I'm certain there are more cases that we don't even know about.

Thompson rubbed his chin thoughtfully as he mulled over Emma's words. He looked down at the note again, as if searching for some hidden meaning within the messy scrawl.

"Alright," he said finally, his skepticism wavering. "What you're saying could have some merit. But we need more than just your observations. Do you have any concrete evidence, anything we can use to expose whoever's behind this?"

Emma hesitated, realizing she hadn't yet uncovered anything substantial. But she was determined to do whatever it took – even if it meant risking her own safety.

"Detective Thompson," she said resolutely, "I don't have hard evidence yet. But I will. And when I do, I need someone willing to listen and help bring this person down."

"Emma," he replied, his voice softening slightly, "your determination is admirable. If you can find me something solid – something we can use to prove there's more to this than just teenage drama – I'll help you get to the bottom of it."

Emma thought about the bloody knife but stopped herself from saying anything about it out loud.

As Emma nodded gratefully, she felt a flicker of hope ignite within her. With Detective Thompson on her side, maybe they stood a chance of unraveling the dark mystery surrounding The Whispering Game.

The late afternoon sun cast elongated shadows across the main street of Crestwood, as Emma and Detective Thompson stood outside Principal Dawson's office. The bustling town atmosphere seemed to buzz around them, oblivious to the sinister undertones that had wormed their way into their lives.

"Alright, Emma," Thompson began, his stern expression betraying a newfound determination. "We need a plan of action. You've been closer to this than I have – any ideas on where to start?"

Emma's mind raced as she considered their options. She recalled the eerie messages she had received and the cryptic clues she had stumbled upon during her investigation.

"Maybe we can start by looking for patterns in the game," she suggested, her blue eyes narrowing with focus. "The players seem to receive strange notes, dares, and challenges. If we can understand how they're being chosen and why, it might lead us to whoever's orchestrating this."

"Good idea," Thompson agreed, nodding thoughtfully. "Have you noticed anything unusual about the notes themselves? Anything that might connect them?"

"Actually, yes," Emma replied, excitement flickering in her eyes as she remembered the details she had painstakingly analyzed. "Some of the notes are written in different handwriting than the others. It's almost like...they were meant to stand out."

"Interesting," Thompson mused, rubbing his chin. "It's possible someone is trying to manipulate the game from within, or perhaps there are multiple people involved. Anything else you've picked up on?"

"Besides the handwriting," Emma continued, "I've also noticed a recurring symbol in some of the clues – a small, stylized eye. It appears in various contexts, but always seems to be linked to key events in the game."

"An eye, huh?" Thompson said, raising an eyebrow. "That could be significant. We'll have to look deeper into that."

As they spoke, Emma could feel the weight of the investigation lifting from her shoulders. With Detective

Thompson by her side, she was no longer alone in her search for answers. Together, they would delve deeper into the darkness and expose the truth behind The Whispering Game.

Detective Thompson's stern face softened as he looked at Emma. "Alright, I'll help you with this. It's clear to me that something nefarious is going on here, and we need to get to the bottom of it."

"Thank you, Detective," Emma breathed out, her heart pounding with renewed purpose.

"Call me Riley," he said, offering a small smile. "Now, let's think about our next steps." The two of them sat down on a nearby bench, surrounded by the bustling energy of Crestwood.

"Okay," Emma began, racking her brain for any potential leads. "We know there are different handwritings on the notes, and that eye symbol keeps reappearing. Maybe we should start by trying to identify who wrote each note?"

"Good idea," Riley agreed. "It might give us an idea of how many people are involved. If we can find some writing samples from the students, maybe we can make a match."

"Principal Dawson could help with that," Emma suggested. "She's bound to have copies of everyone's handwriting from assignments and such."

"True, but we'd need a reason to access those files without raising suspicion," Riley mused, rubbing his chin in thought.

"Maybe we could say it's part of a handwriting analysis project for one of our classes?" Emma offered, her pulse quickening at the thought of their plan taking shape.

Riley nodded in approval. "That could work. We'll need to be careful not to tip our hand, though. If someone involved in the game gets wind of our investigation, they might try to cover their tracks."

"Right," Emma agreed, her blue eyes narrowing with determination. "We also need to look more into that eye symbol. If we can figure out its origin or meaning, it might point us towards whoever's behind all this."

"Agreed," Riley said. "I'll do some research on my end, see if I can find anything about its history or any similar symbols used in the past."

"Great," Emma replied, feeling a sense of camaraderie with the detective. They would face the darkness together and bring an end to The Whispering Game – whatever it took.

"Remember, Emma," Riley cautioned, his voice low and serious. "We're dealing with something dangerous here. Stay vigilant and be careful who you trust."

"I will," she promised, her heart swelling with resolve.

Emma and Detective Thompson stood in the heart of Crestwood, surrounded by a flurry of activity as the townspeople went about their daily routines. The warm sunlight filtered through the canopy of trees lining the streets, casting dappled shadows on the pavement below. Emma felt a newfound sense of hope now that she had the detective on her side.

"Thank you, Detective Thompson," she said softly, her voice nearly lost in the hum of conversation and laughter around them. "I can't tell you how relieved I am to have someone else take this seriously."

"Call me Riley," he replied with a small smile, his stern expression softened by the understanding in his eyes. "We're in this together, Emma. And we'll get to the bottom of it."

"Riley," she repeated, smiling back at him. She glanced around the bustling town, her gaze briefly falling on Principal Dawson as she exited a nearby store, her arms laden with bags.

"Is that your principal?" Riley asked, following Emma's line of sight.

"Principal Eleanor Dawson," Emma confirmed. "She runs the school with an iron fist, but deep down, she really does care about the students."

"Perhaps we should keep her in the loop," Riley suggested. "She might be able to help us in our investigation."

"Maybe," Emma agreed hesitantly, her thoughts racing. "But we need to be careful who we involve. We still don't know who's behind the game or how far-reaching its influence is."

"True," Riley conceded. "For now, let's focus on gathering more information. We can decide later if bringing others into our confidence is necessary."

"Sounds like a plan," Emma said, nodding her agreement as they began to walk along the busy street, side by side. The town seemed to buzz with life all around her, feeling both familiar and foreign at the same time. In the midst of it all, she found solace in knowing she wasn't alone in her quest for answers.

CHAPTER 5

Emma's phone buzzed in her pocket, startling her from her thoughts. She pulled it out and glanced at the screen. An unknown number had sent her a message, containing a task that involved deciphering a complex code.

"Who could this be from?" she muttered to herself, as her deep-set blue eyes scanned the message. The code consisted of seemingly random symbols, each more intricate than the next. It was nothing like anything she had seen before and its complexity intrigued her.

The symbols were arranged in a series of concentric circles, with each circle filled with a different set of characters. Some appeared to be ancient runes, while others looked like mathematical equations or astrological signs. Interspersed among these were tiny images representing various elements - fire, air, earth, water - and what seemed to be representations of celestial bodies.

"Wow," Emma whispered, her fingers tracing the patterns on the screen. "This is insane."

Her curiosity piqued, Emma began to study the code more closely, trying to find any clues or patterns that could help her crack it. But the more she looked, the more impenetrable it seemed.

"Ugh," she groaned, running her fingers through her long chestnut hair. "This is impossible. How am I supposed to figure this out?"

As she continued to stare at the code, frustration mounting, her phone chimed again. Another message from the same unknown number:

"Every symbol has meaning. Look closer."

"Look closer?" Emma repeated, narrowing her eyes to the screen. She took a deep breath and focused, searching for any hidden connections between the symbols, any pattern that might reveal the key to unlocking the code.

"Come on, Emma. Think," she muttered to herself, tapping her fingers against the table as she stared intently at the code. The symbols seemed to dance before her eyes, taunting her with their elusive meanings.

"Ugh!" she groaned, forcefully rubbing her temples. She could feel a headache brewing in her skull. Despite her frustration, Emma's deep-set blue eyes remained locked on the screen, analyzing every detail, searching for any clue that might unravel the mystery.

"Okay, okay," she whispered, trying to calm herself down. "Let's start with the elements. Maybe they're the key."

Her fingers flew over the keyboard, pulling up information on ancient elemental symbols and their possible connections to other systems of knowledge. But for every connection she found, there were twice as many dead ends.

"Stupid code," she hissed under her breath, her hands gripping the edge of the table so tightly her knuckles turned white. The pressure was mounting; she could feel it squeezing her chest, making it difficult to breathe. She couldn't bear the thought of failing this task. She needed to prove herself, to show that she was capable of solving even the most intricate puzzles.

"Think, think, think!" She slammed her fist against the table, causing her laptop to wobble precariously. Her determination burned like a fire within her, refusing to be extinguished by frustration or failure.

"Alright, let's try something else," she said, her voice strained but resolute. "Astrology, maybe?"

She focused on the celestial symbols, trying to discern any patterns or relationships between them that might reveal a hidden message. As her mind raced, she began to jot down potential connections, her pen slashing across the notepad in frantic scribbles.

"Argh! This is driving me insane!" Emma cried, throwing her pen across the room. It bounced off the wall and clattered to the floor, its plastic casing cracking under the impact.

"Deep breaths, Emma. You can do this," she reminded herself, inhaling deeply and exhaling slowly. She couldn't afford to let frustration get the better of her. The code was complex, but she refused to believe it was unsolvable.

"Hey, Emma, need some help?" The sudden voice startled her. She looked up to see Ava Martinez standing in the doorway, her curly black hair framing her sharp brown eyes.

"Uh, sure," Emma replied hesitantly, skeptical of her own abilities at this point.

"Mind if I take a look?" Ava asked as she walked over and pulled up a chair next to Emma. Without waiting for an answer, she leaned in and studied the code intently.

"Wow, this is... intricate," Ava murmured, her eyes darting across the screen. "But I bet we can crack it."

"Really? You think so?" Emma asked, hope flickering in her chest.

"Absolutely," Ava replied confidently. "I've seen worse."

Ava's fingers danced over the keyboard as she accessed various hacking tools and scripts she had developed over the years. "Let's try analyzing the frequency of the symbols first," she suggested, glancing at Emma for approval.

"Sure, go ahead," Emma agreed, intrigued by Ava's approach.

"Okay, notice how some symbols appear much more frequently than others?" Ava pointed out, her eyebrows furrowed in concentration. "That could mean they represent common letters or numbers."

"Right, like E and T in English," Emma caught on, feeling a renewed sense of motivation.

"Exactly!" Ava exclaimed, grinning at their shared understanding. "Now let's see if we can find any patterns within the groups of less frequent symbols."

As the girls began working together, Emma marveled at Ava's expertise and quick thinking. She found herself grateful for the assistance, realizing that cracking this code might not have been possible without Ava's help. As they continued to decipher the cryptic message, Emma felt the weight of her earlier frustration begin to lift, replaced by a growing sense of camaraderie and determination.

"Okay, look here," Ava said, pointing to a cluster of symbols that repeated throughout the code. "Do you think it could be some sort of delimiter?"

"Maybe," Emma replied, her blue eyes narrowing as she studied the pattern. "Or it might be a keyword that unlocks something else."

"True," Ava considered, tapping her index finger against her lips. "Let's try isolating those and see what we find."

"I'll run it through my decryption software," Emma offered, her fingers flying over her keyboard.

As the program worked its magic, the girls leaned forward, anticipation thrumming in the air between them. Suddenly, a series of letters appeared on the screen.

"YES!" Ava exclaimed, pumping her fist in the air. "We're onto something!"

"Okay, but we're not there yet," Emma reminded her, trying to keep her own excitement in check. "What do these letters mean?"

"Could be an anagram," Ava suggested, her voice all business again.

"Or a cipher," Emma mused, running her hand through her chestnut hair.

"Let's test both," Ava proposed, already opening another program on her laptop.

"Wait!" Emma interrupted, her eyes widening. "I think I see something... a pattern within the anagram."

"Really?" Ava asked, swiveling her chair to get a better look. "Show me."

"Here," Emma pointed, tracing her finger along a sequence of letters. "If we rearrange these letters, they spell out a name."

"Whoa," Ava breathed, clearly impressed. "That's clever."

"Very," Emma agreed, feeling a surge of pride at their progress. "But what does this name mean? Is it a person? A place?"

"Could be either," Ava shrugged, her brown eyes thoughtful. "Or maybe it's a clue leading us to the next part of the code."

"Let's keep digging," Emma decided, her determination renewed. "We're getting closer, I can feel it."

"Agreed," Ava nodded, her fingers already flying across her keyboard once more. "Let's crack this thing wide open."

The room was dimly lit, casting eerie shadows on the walls as Emma and Ava huddled around Ava's laptop. Their eyes were strained from hours of poring over the code, but a relentless determination drove them forward.

"Okay, let's try this," Ava muttered, fingers tapping rapidly on the keys. She furrowed her brow in concentration, her curly black hair framing her face as she inputted a new sequence.

"Nothing," Emma sighed, frustration evident in her voice. "We've hit another dead end."

"Dang it." Ava exhaled sharply and leaned back in her chair. "What are we missing?"

"Sometimes... it feels like we're chasing our own tails," Emma admitted, rubbing her temples. "But we can't give up. There has to be something here."

"Right." Ava nodded, her gaze never leaving the screen. "So, we found that name, but what do we do with it?"

"Maybe..." Emma hesitated, her mind racing through possibilities. "Maybe we should look at it from a different angle. What if it's not just a name? What if it's an acronym or an abbreviation?"

"Interesting thought," Ava agreed, leaning forward again. "Let's break it down."

As they dissected the name, trying various combinations and methods, the minutes ticked by, turning into hours. Their eyes grew heavy, their movements sluggish, but they refused to surrender to fatigue.

"Wait!" Emma exclaimed suddenly, her deep-set blue eyes widening. "What if we reverse the letters and use the numbers we found earlier?"

"Could be worth a shot," Ava replied, quickly adjusting the code accordingly. She held her breath as she hit 'enter.'

"Still nothing?" Emma asked, disappointment seeping into her voice.

"No, but... I think we're on the right track," Ava said, scratching her head. "Maybe we need to apply a different algorithm using those reversed letters and numbers."

"Or, what if the code is multilayered?" Emma suggested, her eyes brightening with renewed energy. "We're dealing with a complex puzzle here. It wouldn't be too far-fetched to assume that there's more than one layer to crack."

"Let's run with that," Ava agreed, excitement creeping into her voice.

As they delved deeper into the code, the atmosphere in the room grew tense. Each new attempt brought them closer to the solution but also revealed how intricate the code truly was. Their fingers trembled from exhaustion, their minds swirling with ideas and theories.

"Come on!" Emma whispered under her breath, her heart pounding as she stared at the screen. "We have to be close by now."

"Okay, let's try this approach," Ava said, inputting another sequence of commands.

A moment of silence hung heavy between them, followed by an audible gasp from Ava.

"Emma... look."

Emma stared at the screen, her pulse quickening. The seemingly random symbols and numbers had rearranged themselves into a coherent list of names. Each name was accompanied by an address and a set of coordinates.

"Is this...?" Emma's voice trailed off as her eyes darted between the names, recognition dawning on her face.

"Looks like we've found the other players," Ava confirmed, her eyes wide with awe. "They were all hidden in the code."

"Wait," Emma whispered, her finger hovering over one particular name. "I know some of these people. They're from school, but I never would have guessed they'd be part of something like this."

"Neither would I," Ava agreed, her gaze locked onto another familiar name. "It's unbelievable."

The realization struck them both simultaneously: their classmates – people they saw every day – were part of the mysterious Whispering Game. A tangled web of intrigue surrounded them, and they had only just begun to unravel it.

"Who could have imagined..." Emma murmured, her thoughts racing with the implications of their discovery.

"Whoever designed this code knew what they were doing," Ava said, admiration in her voice. "Keeping the players' identities hidden within layers of encryption... It's genius."

"Genius or not, we've cracked it." Emma couldn't help but feel a surge of pride at their accomplishment. "We have the names, addresses, and coordinates of every player involved in this twisted game."

"Right. Now we need to figure out our next move," Ava said determinedly, her eyes meeting Emma's.

"Agreed. We need to dig deeper, find out why these people are playing and what they hope to gain from it." Emma clenched her fists, resolve filling her chest. "And most importantly, we need to make sure no one else gets hurt."

"Let's do this," Ava said, extending her hand to Emma.

"Deal," Emma responded, grasping Ava's hand firmly. Together, they had accomplished the seemingly impossible task of decoding the hidden message, unmasking the players involved in the Whispering Game. As they exchanged determined looks, they knew that their journey into the heart of this dangerous game had only just begun.

CHAPTER 6

Emma stood alone in the school courtyard, her deep-set blue eyes scanning the bustling scene before her. She could feel the weight of "The Whispering Game" pressing down on her chest like a ton of bricks. Though she had always been independent and resourceful, Emma knew that unraveling the mysteries of this dangerous game would require help. She needed allies, people who could offer unique skills and insights to aid her in her quest for answers. She quickly thought of Lucas, he and Ava had previously worked together on this game. As she walked through the courtyard of the school, her eyes finally found Lucas leaning against a tree.

"Hey, Lucas," she called out as she approached him, her chestnut hair swaying with each determined step.

"Emma?" Lucas replied, pushing himself off the tree with a hint of surprise. "What's up?"

"Can I talk to you? Alone?" Her voice was hushed, almost a whisper, and the urgency in her tone left no room for argument.

"Sure," he said, giving his friends a quick nod before following Emma away from the crowd.

She led him to a secluded corner of the courtyard, the sounds of their classmates' laughter fading into the background. They were alone now, and Emma took a deep breath to steady herself before speaking.

"Lucas, I need your help with something. It's...complicated." The words spilled out of her mouth, revealing her vulnerability for just a brief moment.

"Of course, Emma. What do you need?" Lucas asked, his easy smile replaced by genuine concern as he noticed the gravity of the situation reflected in her eyes.

"Promise me you won't say a word to anyone." Her voice was firm, demanding trust.

"Emma, I promise," he said, his voice steady and sincere.

With that, Emma began to lay out her plan. She would need Lucas to help her navigate the treacherous waters of "The Whispering Game" and the diverse cast of players who inhabited it. Though she was still hesitant to put her faith in others, Emma knew that this uneasy alliance was her best chance at uncovering the truth behind the game. The stakes were high, and time was running out.

"Emma," Lucas hesitated, his easy demeanor crumbling. "I don't know what you're getting into, but if you really believe it's dangerous...I'm in. I can't stand by and let people get hurt."

"Thank you, Lucas," Emma whispered, relief flooding through her. As they stood there, the weight of their decision settling upon them, she couldn't shake the feeling that she had just made the right choice. Lucas's moral compass and intuition would be invaluable in their pursuit of the truth.

"Let's do this," he said, determination glinting in his eyes.

As Emma and Lucas continued their discussion during lunch in the school cafeteria, Emma explained the last puzzle that she and Ava solved. "Let's bring Ava over to our table and discuss this plan together," Emma says. Scanning the cafeteria, Emma finds Ava sitting at a table alone eating lunch.

"Ava," Emma yells from across the room. Ava looks up and sees Emma waving her over to their table.

As the three of them huddled together, poring over the cryptic clues and hidden dangers of The Whispering Game, Emma couldn't help but feel a stirring of hope for the first time in a long while. They were an unlikely team—each harboring their own secrets and fears—but somehow, it felt like they might just have a chance at unraveling the darkness that had ensnared them all.

"Here's what I think," Ava began, her eyes never leaving the screen as she outlined her plan. "We need to be smart about this. No stupid risks."

"Agreed," Emma nodded, her heart pounding with renewed determination. "We'll figure this out. Together."

"Right," Lucas chimed in, his steady presence a comforting reminder of their shared resolve. "Let's do this."

And with that, the three of them embarked on their dangerous journey, bound by a fragile trust and a common goal: to expose the truth behind The Whispering Game and put an end to its deadly reign once and for all.

After school, Emma, Ava and Lucas met back at Emma's house to discuss the plan.

The flickering light from Ava's laptop cast eerie shadows on their faces as they studied the latest challenge set forth by The Whispering Game. Emma felt a chill crawl up her spine, the room suddenly feeling more sinister than before.

"Look at this riddle," Emma said, swallowing the lump in her throat. "It's like it was written in code or something."

"Maybe it was," Ava mused, her brow furrowing as she leaned closer to the screen. "These symbols... I've seen them before."

"Where?" Lucas asked.

"An old book about cryptography," Ava replied, tapping her fingers restlessly on the keyboard. "I'll see if I can find any patterns."

"Good idea," Emma murmured, her mind racing with possibilities. What if they couldn't solve the riddle? What would happen to them?

"Ok, let's think," Lucas interjected, sensing Emma's growing anxiety. "What do we know so far?"

"Players have gone missing," Emma said slowly, her voice barely above a whisper. "I read a news article about it this morning."

"We really need to put our heads together and figure this out," Emma whispered.

"Right," Ava nodded, her eyes narrowing as she continued to analyze the symbols. "So, we need to figure out what these tasks are meant to do, and how to stop them."

"Exactly," Lucas agreed, his steady gaze holding Emma's. "But we can't let fear control us. We need to stay focused and work together."

Emma took a deep breath, drawing strength from Lucas' quiet confidence. He was right; they had to stay strong and united if they wanted to stand a chance against the game's dark forces.

"Alright," Emma said, determination hardening her expression. "Let's break it down. What are the key elements of each task?"

"Symbols, hidden messages, and manipulation," Ava listed off, her fingers flying across the keyboard as she worked. "They're designed to make us question everything, even ourselves."

"Sounds like psychological warfare," Lucas mused.

"Exactly," Ava confirmed. "But if we can anticipate their moves, we can turn the game against them."

"Like chess," Emma added, a spark of hope igniting within her.

"Right," Lucas nodded. "We just have to stay one step ahead."

"Let's start by decoding this riddle, then," Emma suggested, her heart pounding with renewed determination. "Together, we can outsmart them."

"Agreed," Ava said, her eyes blazing with resolve as she cracked her knuckles and returned her focus to the symbols.

As they plunged headfirst into deciphering the riddle, Emma couldn't help but feel an odd sense of camaraderie. Despite their differences, they were united in their quest for answers, bound by the same unyielding desire to bring The Whispering Game to its knees. And though the challenges they faced were daunting, Emma knew that together, they could conquer anything.

The sun dipped below the horizon, casting eerie shadows across the room as Emma, Lucas, and Ava hunched over a piece of paper covered in cryptic symbols. The tense atmosphere was palpable as they worked together, each bringing their unique skills to the table.

"Could this be a Caesar cipher?" Lucas asked, tracing one of the symbols with his finger.

"Or a Vigenère cipher," Ava countered, her eyes narrowing in concentration. "I'll run both through my decryption software."

"Wait," Emma interjected, holding up her hand. "Look at the pattern here." She pointed out a series of symbols that seemed to repeat. "This might be a polyalphabetic substitution cipher."

"Good catch," Lucas nodded, impressed by Emma's keen observation.

"Emma's right," Ava confirmed after running the analysis. "Polyalphabetic it is."

"Okay, so what's the key?" Emma asked, her heart racing with excitement.

"Let me try something," Ava said, typing furiously on her laptop. Moments later, she grinned triumphantly. "Got it! The plaintext message is 'Beware the one who whispers.'"

"Who could that be?" Lucas questioned, a shiver running down his spine.

"Someone we haven't met yet, or maybe someone right under our noses," Emma mused, her blue eyes clouded with suspicion.

"Trust no one," Ava added.

"Agreed," Lucas said solemnly. "Let's keep digging for more clues."

As they continued their investigation, an unspoken bond began to form between them. They were growing to rely on each other's strengths, and their initial reservations about trusting one another slowly faded.

"Wait," Ava said. "Along with the plaintext is what looks like coordinates." A long series of numbers followed the words.

Ava typed in the coordinates into her laptop and gave a frightening look to Emma and Lucas.

"Looks like the coordinates go to an old-looking abandoned warehouse on the outskirts of town," Ava said.

CHAPTER 7

The sun descended, painting the sky with hues of warm amber, and elongating shadows as Emma and her team neared the deserted warehouse. A momentary pause gripped them, their breaths suspended in anticipation as they absorbed the scene unfolding before them.

"Are we certain this is the location?" Emma queried, her chestnut hair dancing across her face in the breeze.

"Absolutely," affirmed Sophie, one of her teammates. "It's precisely where the map directed us."

Emma scrutinized the structure once more, her determined deep-set blue eyes narrowing. The warehouse loomed like a decaying behemoth, its once-stalwart walls now succumbing to the ravages of time. Shattered windows yawned open, resembling jagged teeth in a monstrous grin reveling in the concealed secrets. Vines slithered up the crumbling brick, coiling around rusted pipes like ominous tendrils.

"Alright then," Emma muttered, squaring her shoulders. "Let's unearth what lies within."

As they approached, the air grew colder and denser, pregnant with the hushed tales of the past. The unsettling ambiance crawled beneath Emma's skin, yet she steeled herself, focused on the purpose that propelled them forward. This place held the answers they sought, and fear would not deter their pursuit.

"Quite eerie, isn't it?" Ava whispered, her keen brown eyes surveying the warehouse's foreboding exterior. "But if there are clues inside, we'll uncover them."

"Indeed," concurred Lucas, his sandy hair falling into his eyes as he nodded. "We've traversed too far to turn back now."

Emma glanced at her determined comrades, their resolve kindling her own. Inhaling deeply, she prepared for the revelations that awaited them beyond the heavy doors.

"Let's embark on this journey," she declared resolutely, and united, they swung open the warehouse doors, bracing themselves for the mysteries within.

The sound of creaking hinges filled the air, followed by an eerie silence. As they stepped inside, the faint sound of dripping water echoed through the vast empty space, casting an unsettling ambiance over the scene.

"Ugh," shuddered Sophie, clutching Emma's arm. "It feels like someone's watching us."

"Stay close," Emma instructed her sister, her thoughts racing with the possibilities of what they might uncover. "And keep your eyes peeled for anything out of the ordinary."

"Like what?" asked Sophie, her freckles standing out against her pale face.

"Documents, photographs, anything that might tell us more about the game and its origins," replied Emma, her voice hushed but firm.

"Got it," murmured Ava as she pulled out her flashlight and began to sweep its beam across the room, revealing piles of debris and long-forgotten remnants of the warehouse's past.

The murky shadows clung to the corners of the warehouse, as Emma and her team ventured deeper into the building. Flickering beams of light from their flashlights cut through the darkness, revealing a maze of rooms and hallways that seemed to twist and turn without end.

"Let's split up," suggested Emma, noticing the unease in her friends' expressions. "We'll cover more ground that way."

"Are you sure?" asked Sophie hesitantly, glancing at the others for reassurance.

"Positive," replied Emma with determination, her resolve bolstered by the thought of what they might discover. "Just remember to stay in touch."

With that, they divided themselves into pairs and set off in different directions, the sound of their footsteps echoing throughout the empty space.

"Look at this," whispered Ava to Emma as they entered a room filled with rotting wooden crates. She knelt down and brushed away the cobwebs to reveal a faded label: 'Property of The Whispering Game.'

"Interesting," murmured Emma, her curiosity piqued. "Keep looking."

As they continued to explore the warehouse, the oppressive atmosphere weighed heavily on them, like a suffocating blanket of dust and decay. Yet, despite their growing discomfort, they pressed on, driven by a need to uncover the truth.

"Hey, Em," called Lucas from another room, his voice strained. "I think we found something!"

"Be right there!" shouted Emma, her heartbeat quickening. She and Ava hurried towards the source of the voice, navigating the labyrinthine corridors with growing urgency.

"Check it out," said Lucas, his flashlight illuminating an old metal locker. The door hung open, revealing its contents: a stack of yellowed newspapers, brittle with age.

"Nice find," remarked Emma, carefully extracting one of the papers. As she scanned the headlines, her eyes widened with shock. "Guys, this is huge."

"Emma, what is it?" asked Ava, worry etched on her face.

"Look at the date," Emma whispered, holding up the newspaper for all of them to see. The realization dawned on them simultaneously: they were standing in a place that held secrets long buried, forgotten by all but those who dared to unravel them.

"Let's keep moving," said Emma, her voice tinged with excitement and fear. "We're getting closer."

A shaft of moonlight pierced the darkness, casting an eerie glow on the far wall. Emma's flashlight flickered across a weathered wooden door barely hanging on its hinges, its paint cracked and peeling.

"Let's see what's behind here," Emma whispered, leading her team towards the door.

"Careful," warned Lucas, extending an arm to steady her as she pushed the door open with a creak that echoed like a scream through the warehouse.

"Thanks." Emma nodded, her heart pounding with anticipation. She stepped into the dimly lit room, her breath catching in her throat at the sight before her.

"Whoa," Ava breathed, following closely behind.

The walls were covered in faded photos and maps, linked together by strings like a spider's web. A large, worn table stood in the center of the room, strewn with frayed books, notebooks, and crumpled papers.

"Look at this," Emma said, picking up a tattered document from the table. Her eyes scanned the words, widening with each line she read.

"Em?" Lucas asked, sensing her excitement.

"It's... it's about the game," she stuttered, disbelief etched on her face. "This is a list of people who played before us. And their fates."

"Are you serious?" Ava asked, shocked.

"Deadly serious," Emma confirmed, handing the document to Lucas. "Some of them... some of them didn't make it out alive."

"Then we have to find out why," Lucas said, determination burning in his eyes. "We can't let that happen to any of us."

"Agreed," Emma said, her resolve strengthened by her friends' support. "We're onto something big here. Let's keep looking."

"Right behind you," Ava whispered, her own fear replaced by the thrill of discovery. Together, they delved deeper into the dark secrets of the Whispering Game, each clue leading them closer to the heart of the mystery.

"Guys, look at this," Emma said, pointing to a date on the document. "This game has been going on for decades."

"Decades?" Ava gulped, her voice barely audible.

"Seems like it," Lucas replied, running his fingers over the list of names. "But why? What's the point?"

"Maybe it's some kind of initiation test," Emma suggested, her brows furrowing in thought. "For what, though? A secret society?"

"Or maybe someone is just really bored and twisted," Ava added, shivering at the thought.

"Whatever it is," Emma said, determination steeling her voice, "we need to put an end to it, and make sure no one else gets hurt."

"Agreed," Lucas nodded. "So, where do we start?"

"Let's keep searching this room," Emma instructed. "There must be more clues here."

As they scoured the room, their eyes fell upon an old photograph, yellowed with age, tucked beneath a pile of papers. Emma picked it up and studied the faces staring back at her. The group in the picture was made up of young people, their expressions a mix of excitement and fear, as if they knew the danger that lay ahead.

"Is this... us?" Ava asked, disbelief coloring her words.

"Can't be," Lucas countered, squinting at the image. "That photo is way too old."

"Look at the back," Emma whispered, her heart pounding as she flipped the photograph. Scrawled in faded ink were the words: 'The first players - may they find redemption.'

"Redemption..." Lucas mused. "From what?"

"Maybe from the game itself," Emma suggested, her mind racing with possibilities. "Could it be that the players are chosen because they need some sort of... atonement?"

"Or maybe they're chosen to help others find redemption," Ava added, her eyes wide with realization. "Maybe that's the point of it all."

"Whatever it is," Emma said, gripping the photograph tightly, "I can't shake the feeling that we're just scratching the surface of something much bigger than us."

"Then let's dig deeper," Lucas declared, his voice resolute. "We'll figure this out together and put an end to the Whispering Game for good."

"Agreed," Emma and Ava echoed in unison, their determination unwavering as they delved further into the warehouse's hidden secrets.

The implications of the photograph weighed heavily on their minds, casting a shadow of uncertainty over their mission. The air seemed to grow colder, each breath now visible as a foggy mist.

"Guys," Emma murmured, her voice barely audible above the dripping water. "There's no turning back now. We need to stay focused and keep our eyes open for anything that might help us understand this game."

"Right," Ava agreed, steeling herself against the fear that had begun to take root in her heart.

"Emma's right. Let's keep moving," Lucas chimed in, determination evident in his steady gaze.

They continued to explore the warehouse, navigating through dimly lit hallways and past concrete pillars that loomed like ancient sentinels. In one corner, they found a tattered journal with entries detailing the experiences of previous players, the words trembling with desperation and regret. They exchanged uneasy glances, knowing that these people had faced the same treacherous path they now walked.

"Listen to this," Emma said, reading from the brittle pages. "'Day 5 - The whispers are getting louder, harder to resist. I can feel my grip on reality slipping away. I don't know how much longer I can hold on.'"

"Five days? That's all it took?" Ava asked, her voice strained.

"Apparently," Lucas replied grimly. "And we've been playing for...?"

"Three," Emma whispered, her hands shaking as she clutched the journal. "We're on day three."

"Okay, we need to find more answers," Lucas insisted, his face pale but resolute. "Let's split up. We'll cover more ground that way."

"Split up?" Ava hesitated, looking at the dark corners of the warehouse and the shadows that seemed to reach out toward them.

"Stay close enough to hear each other," Lucas suggested, sensing her unease. "But far enough apart to explore different areas."

"Alright," Emma agreed, nodding at Ava for reassurance. "Let's do this."

As they spread out, their footsteps echoed throughout the warehouse, a constant reminder of the solitude that threatened to engulf them. The weight of their task bore down on their shoulders as they searched for any clue that could provide insight into the mysterious game.

It was Ava who found the next piece of the puzzle: an old newspaper article about a group of teenagers who had vanished without a trace decades ago. Their faces mirrored those in the photograph, their eyes filled with the same mix of excitement and terror.

"Emma, Lucas, look at this!" Ava called, her voice trembling with urgency.

"Those are the same people from the photo," Emma realized, her blue eyes widening as she scanned the article.

"Players before us... They disappeared," Lucas whispered, his words heavy with implication. "Do you think...?"

"Maybe," Emma said quietly, her mind racing with possibilities. "The game has been going on for longer than we thought, and it's claimed lives before."

"Then we need to put an end to it," Ava asserted, her voice echoing through the empty space. "Not just for ourselves, but for everyone who's played before us."

"Agreed," Emma said, determination hardening her features. "We'll find the truth behind the Whispering Game and make sure no one else falls victim to its deadly whispers."

"Guys, let's try to find a pattern," Lucas suggested, wiping the sweat from his forehead as they continued to move through the warehouse. "There must be a common thread that ties all the players together."

"Great idea," Ava chimed in, her fingers tracing the outline of a faded symbol etched into the wall. "Any thoughts?"

"Let's see if we can find more clues that point to the game's origins," Emma urged, an unwavering determination in her eyes. "If we can understand where it came from, maybe we'll have a better chance of stopping it."

As they delved further into the dark recesses of the warehouse, each new discovery seemed to raise more questions than answers. The air grew colder, the shadows longer, and the silence more oppressive.

"Look at this!" Ava exclaimed, holding up a tattered journal. Its pages were filled with frantic scribbles and cryptic symbols, the ink smudged and faded with age. "It's like someone was trying to document their experiences with the game."

"Could it be one of the previous players?" Lucas pondered, his brow furrowed in concentration as he examined the worn cover.

"Maybe," Emma replied, her heart pounding in her chest as she gingerly flipped through the pages. "We need to study this closely. It could hold vital information about the game's inner workings."

"Emma's right," Ava agreed, her eyes scanning the journal's contents with a fervent intensity. "We can't let the game claim any more lives."

"Let's take this back to the others and see what they think," Emma suggested, her grip tightening on the journal as if it were their lifeline out of the darkness that surrounded them.

As they turned to leave the warehouse, a sudden gust of wind blew through the shattered windows, sending chills down their spines. The shadows seemed to dance mockingly on the walls, taunting them with the knowledge that they had only just begun to uncover the secrets of the Whispering Game.

CHAPTER 8

Emma's fingers drummed against the table, her deep-set blue eyes flicking between the computer screen and Ava's retreating figure. The fiery hacker mumbled an excuse about needing air before slipping out of their makeshift headquarters, leaving Emma with a gnawing suspicion that something wasn't right.

"Where are you going, Ava?" she called after her, but the door slammed shut before she could get an answer.

Ava had been acting strangely for days now, her usual no-nonsense attitude replaced by evasiveness and sudden disappearances. As much as Emma wanted to trust her friend, the feeling that Ava was hiding something grew stronger with each passing moment. Jake, a fellow teammate, who also knows Ava well may know more about why she is acting so strange.

"Hey, Em," Jake said, entering the room with a plate of sandwiches. "You okay?"

"Fine," Emma replied, forcing a smile. But her thoughts were elsewhere, her curiosity getting the better of her as she pondered Ava's behavior.

"Has Ava mentioned anything to you lately?" she asked casually, taking a bite of her sandwich

"Like what?" Jake shrugged, his mouth full. "She's just been... Ava."

But Emma knew better. She couldn't shake the feeling that something was off, and it threatened to consume her every thought.

As soon as Jake left the room, Emma sprang into action. Her heart hammered in her chest as she approached Ava's desk, scanning the cluttered surface for any clues or evidence of her possible betrayal.

"Come on, Ava," she whispered to herself, her hands trembling slightly as they hovered over the keyboard. "What are you hiding?"

She knew it was wrong to go through her friend's things, but the need for answers was too great. With each passing second, Emma's determination to uncover the truth intensified. Whatever secret Ava was keeping, she needed to know.

Her fingers danced across the keys, searching through files and emails, looking for any sign that Ava was not the ally she claimed to be. It was a race against time, as Emma knew Ava could return at any moment.

"Please," she thought, her chest tightening with anxiety. "Please let me find something."

And then, there it was - a hidden folder, tucked away between work projects and personal photos. Emma hesitated for a moment, knowing that what she found inside could change everything. But she had come too far to turn back now.

"Forgive me, Ava," she murmured, double-clicking on the folder and bracing herself for what she might discover.

The screen illuminated with a series of cryptic messages, timestamped from just days prior. Emma's pulse quickened as she read through them, noticing discrepancies between what Ava had told her and the conversations displayed before her.

"Emma?" Ava's voice sliced through the quiet room like a knife, causing Emma to jump and slam the laptop closed in panic.

"Hey," Emma said, trying to keep her voice steady. Her chestnut hair fell into her face, and she brushed it back nervously. "I was just... looking for something."

"Did you find what you were looking for?" Ava asked, her usually warm brown eyes narrowed in suspicion.

"Actually," Emma said, taking a deep breath. "There's something I wanted to talk to you about."

Ava crossed her arms over her chest, her tough exterior on full display. "What's up?"

"Remember when you said you were at the library last Saturday?" Emma started, trying to sound casual. She fiddled with a loose thread on her shirt, unable to meet Ava's gaze. "I was there too, but I didn't see you."

"Maybe we just missed each other," Ava replied coolly, her fingers drumming against her arm. "The library is pretty big, after all."

"Right," Emma agreed, biting her lip. "But then, yesterday, you said you were working on that new algorithm all night. Yet, I saw you leave the building around eight o'clock."

"Maybe I needed a break," Ava retorted sharply, her eyes flashing with annoyance. "Is it a crime to step out for some fresh air?"

"No, of course not," Emma said quickly, her heart pounding in her ears. "It's just... these inconsistencies are making me wonder if there's something you're not telling me."

"Like what?" Ava snapped, her body tensing as if preparing for a fight.

"Look, I don't know," Emma admitted, her voice barely above a whisper. "But something's not adding up, and I need to know if I can trust you."

"Trust me?" Ava scoffed, her eyes filling with hurt and anger. "You're the one going through my things!"

"Because I'm worried about you!" Emma cried out, finally meeting Ava's gaze head-on. "I thought we were in this together. But it feels like you're hiding something from me, and it's tearing me apart."

Ava stared at Emma for a long moment, her jaw clenched as she seemed to wrestle with herself. Finally, she let out a deep breath, her shoulders slumping in defeat.

"Tell me," Emma pleaded, a mix of relief and dread washing over her. "Please, just tell me the truth."

"Fine," Ava spat, her voice tense and guarded. "You think I'm hiding something? Go ahead, ask me anything."

"Alright," Emma said, swallowing hard. "Why were you meeting with that man in the alley?"

"I told you, he was just a contact. Someone who could get us information," Ava replied defensively, her eyes darting away from Emma's probing gaze.

"Then why did it look like you were exchanging something with him?" Emma pressed on, remembering the shadowy figure she had seen Ava meet earlier.

"Information needs to be exchanged somehow, doesn't it?" Ava retorted, but the slight tremble in her voice betrayed her unease.

"Okay, then explain this," Emma continued, her resolve growing stronger as she held up a cryptic message she had found among Ava's belongings. "This looks like a coded message from the Mastermind."

Ava's eyes widened for a moment before her expression hardened, bitterness twisting her features. "So now I'm working with the enemy? Is that what you think?"

"Is it true?" Emma persisted, feeling a knot of anxiety tighten in her stomach.

"Absolutely not!" Ava declared, her voice shaking with emotion. "I would never betray you or our cause, Emma. You know that."

"Then why didn't you tell me about any of this?" Emma asked softly, her anger dissolving into hurt. "We're supposed to be a team."

"Because... because I didn't want to scare you," Ava confessed, her voice cracking under the weight of her secret. "I thought I could handle it on my own and keep you safe."

"Safe from what?" Emma inquired, her confusion deepening as Ava hesitated, seemingly on the verge of breaking down.

"From... from the Mastermind," Ava finally admitted, tears streaming down her cheeks as the awful truth spilled out. "They contacted me, Emma. They knew things about me, about my family. They threatened to hurt them if I didn't cooperate."

"Cooperate?" Emma echoed, the word feeling like a punch to the gut. "So, you've been working with them all along?"

"I had no choice!" Ava sobbed, her shoulders shaking as she struggled to explain herself. "I didn't game to betray you, but they... they forced me into it. I didn't know what else to do."

As Ava's confession hung heavy in the air, Emma felt a storm of emotions raging within her, threatening to tear her apart. But despite the crushing weight of Ava's betrayal, she couldn't help but feel a flicker of empathy for the girl who had been manipulated by the Mastermind all along.

Emma stared at Ava, her heart pounding in her chest like a jackhammer as she struggled to make sense of the words that had just left her friend's mouth. Her mind raced with conflicting emotions – anger at the betrayal, hurt that someone she trusted could do this, and yet, an underlying understanding of the impossible position Ava had been placed in.

"Was it all a lie then?" Emma asked quietly, her voice trembling with barely contained emotion. "Every mission we went on together, every late-night strategy session, every laugh we shared... was it all just part of your act?"

Ava's eyes filled with tears, her lower lip quivering as she shook her head vehemently. "No, Emma, I swear. Our friendship was real, is real. I never meant for any of this to happen. It just... it spiraled out of control."

"Out of control?" Emma scoffed, feeling the heat of her own rage bubbling beneath the surface. "You helped the very person who's been tormenting us! How could you?"

"Because I was scared!" Ava cried out, her voice breaking. "I thought I could protect my family by doing what they asked, but I didn't realize how deep I was getting."

"Scared?" Emma's voice cracked. "What about me, Ava? What about the rest of the team? Did you ever think about how scared we were when everything started falling apart around us?"

"Of course, I did!" Ava snapped, her guilt turning into frustration. "Don't you think I hated myself for what I was doing? The sleepless nights, the constant fear of being found out... it was tearing me apart, Emma!"

"Then why didn't you come to us?" Emma implored, her eyes pleading with Ava for some semblance of reason. "We could have helped you, figured something out. But instead, you chose to deceive us."

"Because I didn't want to drag you guys down with me!" Ava's voice shook, her tears now flowing freely. "I was trying to protect you. I never wanted any of this."

"Protect us?" Emma spat, the feeling of betrayal weighing heavily on her heart. "By lying to us and working with our enemy? Some protection that is."

Ava flinched as if she had been slapped, the pain of Emma's words cutting deep. She looked at her friend with tearful eyes, searching for forgiveness in a place where it seemed unreachable.

"Emma," she whispered, her voice barely audible amidst the storm of emotions that filled the room. "I'm so sorry. If I could go back and change everything, I would. But I can't. All I can do now is try to make things right."

"Then prove it," Emma said, her voice cold and unyielding. "Help us take down the Mastermind once and for all."

Ava took a deep breath, her eyes locked on Emma's as she began to explain. "When I first found out about the Mastermind, I was just trying to figure out what they were up to. But they caught me snooping around, and they... threatened my family, Emma. I couldn't risk their safety." Ava's hands trembled as she spoke; it was clear that she was sharing with Emma her most guarded secrets.

"Go on," Emma urged, her voice wavering.

"From there, things escalated quickly. The Mastermind forced me to work for them, to use my skills against you and the others. They always seemed one step ahead of me, like they knew exactly how to keep me under their control." Ava's eyes clouded over, haunted by memories of the past.

"Did they ever hurt your family?" Emma asked, her heart aching at the thought.

"Thankfully, no. But the fear was always there, hanging over me like a shadow. It was a constant reminder that I had no choice but to obey."

Emma could hear the anguish in Ava's voice, and despite her anger, she felt a wave of empathy wash over her. She knew all too well the lengths people would go to protect the ones they loved. And now, she realized that Ava was just another pawn in the Mastermind's twisted game, manipulated into betraying her friends and herself.

"Emma," Ava said hesitantly, breaking the silence that had settled between them. "Do you think you could ever forgive me?"

Emma looked deep into Ava's pleading eyes. She knew that forgiveness wouldn't come easily, but she also understood that holding onto resentment would only make things worse. What they needed now was unity, not division.

"Maybe not right away, Ava" Emma admitted, swallowing the lump in her throat. "But we're going to fight back, together. We're going to take down the Mastermind and make sure they can never hurt anyone else again."

"Thank you," Ava whispered, her eyes glistening with unshed tears. "I promise I'll do everything in my power to make things right."

"Good," Emma said resolutely. "Now let's get to work."

CHAPTER 9

The shadows of the towering trees cast eerie shapes against the moonlit ground as Emma and her team huddled in the secluded clearing. Her chestnut hair hung loosely around her shoulders, her deep-set blue eyes flicking between each of her fellow players with a mix of suspicion and determination. She clutched a tattered notebook tightly to her chest, the pages filled with cryptic clues and hastily scribbled connections.

"Alright," she whispered, her voice barely audible above the rustling leaves. "Let's go over everything again. We need to be ready for whatever the Mastermind throws at us."

Ava nodded, her brow furrowed in concentration as she flipped open her own notebook. "We've got the list of victims, their time of disappearance, and what we think are the locations where they were taken."

"Good," Emma replied, scanning the notes one more time. "And Lucas, you found that pattern with the numbers, right?"

"Right," Lucas confirmed, his voice tense. "It seems like the Mastermind is using some kind of code to communicate with the other players. Whenever someone new joins the game, they're given a number. That number corresponds to a specific location or task they have to complete."

"Which means," Emma mused, her mind racing with possibilities, "that if we can crack the code, we might be able to predict the Mastermind's next move."

"Exactly," Ava chimed in, her excitement palpable. "We just need to figure out how the numbers tie into the bigger picture."

Emma chewed on her bottom lip, her thoughts swirling like a storm inside her head. What was the purpose of this twisted game? Why were they all being drawn into its web of deceit and danger? And most importantly, who was the Mastermind pulling the strings behind the scenes?

"Guys, I think there's something else we're missing," Emma said slowly, her eyes narrowing as she stared at the pages before her. "There has to be a reason why we were all chosen to play this game. What do we have in common?"

"Besides being teenagers with too much time on our hands?" Lucas muttered dryly, but his eyes held a glimmer of curiosity.

"Consider this," Emma urged, her tone intensifying. "We've all become targets of the Mastermind for some reason. There must be a common thread linking us."

A hush settled over the group, each member engrossed in their own thoughts, attempting to unveil the concealed connection. The wind howled through the overhead trees, sending chills down their spines and emphasizing the gravity of the situation.

Standing beneath the moonlight, the puzzle pieces gradually fell into place. Emma sensed they were on the verge of uncovering the truth about the Whispering Game and the enigmatic puppeteer orchestrating it from the shadows.

The moon cast an eerie glow, creating haunting shadows on the forest floor. The air buzzed with anticipation as Emma scrutinized the evidence laid out before her.

"Okay," she declared, standing upright and addressing the team. "We know there's a link between all of us. Perhaps revisiting the warehouse will reveal more clues about why we were chosen for this game."

Lucas hesitated, his brow furrowed. "Emma, what if it's a trap? The Mastermind knows we're onto them."

Emma took a deep breath, her chestnut hair cascading over her determined face. "I understand the risks, but sitting idle won't help. We need to be proactive. I believe the answer lies somewhere in that warehouse."

"Fine," Lucas sighed, nervously running his sandy hair through his fingers. "Let's go back, but we'll be cautious, alright?"

"Of course," Emma affirmed, her blue eyes resolute. As they prepared to depart, her mind raced with uncertainties. Was she leading them into danger, or was she unraveling the secret behind the Whispering Game?

Soon, the team found themselves outside the dilapidated warehouse, exploring for fresh clues.

"Stay close," she whispered to Lucas as they slipped through the darkness. The abandoned structure loomed ahead, its shattered windows resembling the maw of a long-forgotten creature. They approached with caution, hearts pounding in their chests.

"Be careful," Lucas murmured, his hand instinctively reaching for hers. Together, they stepped into the decaying building, the smell of damp and rotting wood filling their nostrils.

"Let's start searching," Emma instructed, pulling out a flashlight. Her resolve grew stronger as they combed every corner of the warehouse, leaving no stone unturned. They needed to find the missing piece of the puzzle – the key that would unlock the truth about the Mastermind and their twisted game.

"Emma?" Lucas whispered, his voice tense. "I trust you, but I can't shake the feeling that we're walking into a trap."

"Lucas," Emma said, meeting his worried gaze. "We have to try something. Anything is better than just waiting for the Mastermind to make their next move."

They had to find the truth. And they would do whatever it took to end the Whispering Game once and for all.

Emma's fingers trembled as she zipped up her jacket, the brisk autumn air swirling around them. "Ava's right," she said, her voice barely audible above the rustle of leaves. "We need more information before we confront the Mastermind."

"Let's go back outside and discuss this before we move any further into this place. We're not sure what we are even looking for at this point," Lucas said.

"Agreed," Ava chimed in, a determined glint in her brown eyes. "We should reach out to our network of players. They might have crucial intel that could help us."

"We are going to need Detective Thompson's help on this," stated Emma. "There is no way that the other players in this game are just going to hand over information to us willingly."

Emma pulled out her phone and called Detective Thompson. "We have more information regarding the game and we need your help. We are outside of the abandoned warehouse."

"Detective Thompson said wait here and don't do anything until he gets here," instructed Emma.

Following Detective Thompson's arrival, Emma lays out all the information they have discovered so far. Emma explained that the group had found players of the game who stated they may have insider information about who was behind all this.

"Alright, let's divide the tasks," Emma instructed, her mind racing. "Lucas, you and I will head back into the abandoned warehouse. Ava, can you and Detective Thompson meet with that player who claims to have insider knowledge?"

"Got it," Ava replied, already pulling out her phone to make arrangements.

"Be careful, both of you," Lucas warned, his sandy hair ruffling in the wind. He squeezed Emma's hand, a silent promise of support.

"Always," Emma whispered, a small smile playing on her lips. She knew they were walking a dangerous path, but they had come too far to turn back now.

"Let's move out," Detective Thompson barked, sliding behind the wheel of his car. Ava climbed in beside him, her curls bouncing as she adjusted her seatbelt.

"Stay in touch," Emma called after them, watching as their car disappeared down the road. Then, turning to Lucas, she added, "Come on, let's not waste any time."

As they stood outside of the warehouse, Emma couldn't help but feel a pang of trepidation. What if Lucas was right? What if this was all just a trap?

But deep down, her instincts told her that the truth lay within those crumbling walls. And she was determined to find it.

"Okay," Lucas murmured, his blue eyes scanning the warehouse's shadowy interior. "Let's do this."

"Let's," Emma agreed, her chestnut hair whipping around her face as they stepped into the darkness. The weight of their mission settled heavily on her shoulders, but she knew that they couldn't turn back now.

"Stay close," Lucas whispered, reaching for her hand. As they moved deeper into the warehouse, Emma found herself grateful for his presence, his warmth a reminder that they weren't alone in this fight.

Together, they would end the Whispering Game – whatever the cost.

The air inside the warehouse was thick with dust and secrets. Emma's heart raced as she and Lucas began their search, his hand still clasped in hers.

"Emma, let's split up," Lucas suggested, his voice barely above a whisper. "We'll cover more ground that way."

"Alright, but be careful," she replied, her blue eyes locking onto his for a moment before they separated.

Emma sifted through piles of debris, her fingers tracing grooves and markings on the walls, searching for anything that might betray the Mastermind's plans. As she moved further into the shadows, she couldn't shake the nagging feeling that they were being watched.

"Lucas," she called out, "I think I found something."

"Me too," he responded, emerging from the darkness with a triumphant grin. "There's a hidden compartment behind this shelf."

"Great, let's see what's inside." Emma approached the shelf, her chestnut hair falling into her face as she examined its contents. She pulled out a tattered note with a cryptic message scrawled across it. "What do you think this means?"

"Hard to say," Lucas admitted, his keen intuition working overtime. "Let's take a photo and show Ava later. She'll know what to do with it."

"Good idea," Emma said, snapping a quick picture of the note on her phone.

—-

Across town, Ava and Detective Thompson met with the player who claimed to have insider knowledge about the game. The young man sat nervously on the park bench, wringing his hands together.

"Tell us everything you know," Detective Thompson urged, his stern expression unyielding. "Time is running out."

"Okay, okay," the player stammered, taking a deep breath. "The game is not what you think...it's not just about playing with our lives. It's about framing all of us for crimes we didn't commit."

Ava's brown eyes narrowed skeptically. "What kind of crimes?"

"Murder, theft, arson, you name it," the player continued, his voice trembling. "The Mastermind is using us as pawns to cover their own tracks. The police questioned me recently about a burglary at a convenience store, they said they had my fingerprints. I told them that I snuck into the back room there a day earlier looking for a clue to the game, but I didn't steal anything. They didn't seem to believe me."

The player went on to say, "My friend was recently arrested for arson. Witnesses say they saw him leaving an abandoned building soon before it caught fire. He too told police that he was there looking for a clue in the game, but they arrested him anyway. I didn't think anyone would believe me, until you contacted me."

"Unbelievable," Ava muttered, her jaw clenched with anger. "I can't believe this is happening."

"Where's your proof?" Detective Thompson demanded, unwilling to take the information at face value.

"Here," the player said, producing a thumb drive from his pocket. "It contains all the evidence I could find. Please, you have to stop them."

"Thank you," Ava said, snatching the drive from his hand. Her mind raced with the implications, her instincts telling her that the information was genuine.

"Emma needs to know about this," she said, already composing a message on her phone. The urgency of the situation weighed heavily upon them; they had to act fast if they hoped to expose the Mastermind and clear their names.

—

In the dimly lit warehouse, Emma and Lucas hunched over the cryptic message, their breaths fogging up in the cold air.

"Looks like some sort of code," Lucas muttered, running a finger along the jumble of letters and numbers. "What do you think?"

Emma's blue eyes narrowed as her mind raced through possible combinations. "It might be an address – a location."

"Can you crack it?" Lucas asked, his voice tinged with both anticipation and concern.

"Watch me," Emma replied, determination etched into every line of her face.

Minutes ticked by, each one stretching out like an eternity. The tension in the air was palpable, the weight of their mission bearing down on them.

"Got it!" Emma exclaimed, triumphantly straightening up. "I knew it!"

"Where does it lead?" Lucas asked, his own excitement bubbling over.

"An old library downtown," she said, her gaze locked onto the decoded message. "We have to go there, now."

"Let's hope this is what we need to expose the Mastermind," Lucas murmured, his easygoing demeanor betraying the anxiety he felt.

"Only one way to find out," Emma replied, already heading towards the exit.

Emma's heart raced as they neared the library, her thoughts consumed by all the potential horrors that awaited them. The Mastermind's game had already taken so much from them; she couldn't let it claim any more victims.

"Stay focused," she told herself, feeling Lucas's reassuring presence beside her. "Together, we'll bring this monster down."

The old library loomed ominously before them, its decaying facade casting eerie shadows on the cracked pavement. Emma's pulse raced as she exchanged a glance with Lucas, her eyes conveying both determination and fear.

Inside, the library was consumed by darkness, the air thick with dust and long-held secrets. They flicked their flashlights on and began to search, their footsteps echoing through the cavernous space.

"Emma, over here!" Lucas called out suddenly, his beam of light revealing an inconspicuous door hidden behind a toppled bookcase.

Emma rushed over, her heart pounding. "Do you think it's—"

"Only one way to find out," Lucas interrupted, pushing the door open with a creak.

A slow, cautious step led them into a hidden room, its walls lined with incriminating evidence against them: photos, newspaper clippings, and documents all carefully compiled to frame them as criminals.

"Unbelievable," Emma breathed, anger surging through her veins. "We've got to document everything, now."

"Agreed," Lucas said, already snapping photos with his phone. "No time to waste."

As they worked, Emma couldn't help but wonder how deep the Mastermind's deception went. How many lives had been ruined by this twisted game?

"Emma, focus," she scolded herself mentally, desperation clawing at her insides.

As Emma and Lucas finished documenting the hidden room's contents, an overwhelming sense of urgency gripped them both.

"Time's running out," Emma whispered, her blue eyes meeting Lucas's gaze. "We need to regroup, share our findings, and take down the Mastermind once and for all."

"Right behind you," Lucas affirmed, his loyalty never wavering. Together, they stepped back into the darkness, armed with the evidence that could change everything.

Emma's phone buzzed, the sound echoing through the dark warehouse. She glanced at the screen, her heart racing as she read Ava's message. Her face quickly went pale as the words shocked her to the core.

"Lucas, there's more to this game than we thought," Emma whispered urgently. "The Mastermind's been framing people."

As they hurried back to their meeting point, Emma couldn't help but think of all the innocent people caught in the crossfire of this twisted game. It was a heavy burden on her shoulders, one that she knew she had to bear.

"Stay focused, Emma," she reminded herself, determination burning within her. "We'll expose the Mastermind and clear everyone's name."

"Emma! Lucas!" Ava called out, her voice tense, as they approached the rendezvous location.

"Right here," Emma replied, her chest heaving from the sprint. Detective Thompson stood beside Ava, his jaw clenched, eyes full of resolve.

"Tell us what you found," Thompson demanded, his stern gaze fixed on Emma and Lucas.

"Hidden room," Lucas panted, catching his breath. "Filled with...incriminating evidence against us."

"Unbelievable," Thompson muttered, frustration etching lines onto his face.

"Enough talk," Emma declared, her blue eyes blazing with determination. "It's time to take action. We need to expose the Mastermind and take our lives back."

"Agreed," Ava said, her fiery spirit shining through. "We won't let them win."

"Count me in," Lucas added, his loyalty unwavering.

"Alright," Thompson conceded, giving them each a nod. "Let's bring this monster down."

As they shared the evidence they'd gathered, the gravity of the situation weighed on them all. But in that moment, they were united – determined to expose the Mastermind and clear their names. And with that shared resolve, there was no obstacle they couldn't overcome.

A chill wind swept through the air, rustling the leaves beneath their feet as they huddled together in the dimly lit alley. Emma's heart raced, her breath forming clouds of vapor. She clenched her fists, steadying herself for what was to come.

CHAPTER 10

The flickering candlelight danced across Emma's face, casting eerie shadows on the walls of her dimly lit room. Her deep-set blue eyes were filled with determination as she stared at her laptop screen, vowing to uncover the truth about the Mastermind and their twisted game. There had been too many sleepless nights, too many unanswered questions that gnawed at her soul.

"Enough," she muttered under her breath, fingers flying across the keyboard as she began her research.

Emma's fingertips clicked and clacked as she delved into the depths of the internet. Social media profiles were scoured, public records sifted through with a fine-tooth comb. She knew that somewhere within this endless sea of information, a glimpse of the Mastermind's past would be hidden.

"Come on, there must be something," she whispered, her voice barely audible above the hum of her computer fan.

Her chestnut hair fell over her shoulder as she leaned in closer to the screen, squinting at the tiny text that filled each page. The hours ticked by, yet no trace of the elusive Mastermind was found. Frustration simmered beneath her skin, threatening to boil over.

"Ugh, this is impossible!" Emma groaned aloud, slamming her palms down onto the desk.

Still, she refused to give up. Her resilience and unwavering commitment to uncovering the truth drove her forward, even as exhaustion weighed heavy on her eyelids.

"Maybe... just one more search," she mumbled, typing in a new set of keywords.

As the results loaded, Emma's heart skipped a beat – buried between mundane articles and irrelevant forum posts, a single headline caught her eye.

"Could this be it?" she asked herself, clicking on the link with cautious optimism.

"Finally," she breathed, as she began to read the contents of the article. A sense of urgency filled her, knowing that every moment spent uncovering the Mastermind's past was a moment closer to danger. But she couldn't stop now.

"Alright, Mastermind," Emma whispered, her voice filled with determination. "Let's see who you really are."

Emma's fingers danced across the keyboard, her eyes darting back and forth between multiple browser tabs. She had been at it for hours, sifting through countless posts, articles and profiles, each promising a lead, only to end in disappointment.

"Ugh!" she groaned, pushing her chair back and burying her face in her hands. It was as if the Mastermind had anticipated every move, leaving a breadcrumb trail of false information that led nowhere.

"Emma, are you okay?" came a voice from the doorway.

"Fine," she muttered, frustrated tears welling up in her eyes. "Just... hitting dead ends."

"Maybe take a break? You've been at this all day," the voice suggested.

"Can't. Need to find something," she mumbled, determination driving her forward.

"Alright, but don't forget to eat something," the voice replied before fading away, leaving Emma alone once more.

She returned to her search, clicking on yet another link that claimed to have insider knowledge of the Mastermind. Expecting another disappointment, her heart raced when she saw a single line of text, hidden in plain sight.

"Hidden truths lie where whispers converge..."

"Whispers?" Emma repeated, her mind racing. Was this a clue? A message left by someone who knew the truth?

"Where whispers converge... Converge..." she murmured, her fingers flying over the keys as she searched for any mention of convergence and whispers. An obscure corner of the internet appeared on her screen, an invitation-only forum titled, "The Whisperers' Den."

"Finally," she whispered, her pulse quickening. Was this where the players of the Whispering Game gathered to discuss its origins?

"Password required" popped up on the screen, forcing Emma to think quickly. She typed in the cryptic message: "Hidden truths lie where whispers converge" and hit enter.

"Access granted."

"Gotcha," Emma muttered, her eyes scanning through post after post discussing the game, its players, and most importantly, the Mastermind. Her frustration began to fade as a sense of accomplishment washed over her. She was one step closer to uncovering the truth.

"Let's see what you're hiding, Mastermind," she whispered, delving deeper into the forum. Little did she know, her determination had now put her on the Mastermind's radar, but it was too late to turn back. The game was just beginning.

The dim glow of the computer screen illuminated Emma's face as she scrolled through the forum dedicated to the

Whispering Game. Avatars and usernames flashed by each representing a player who had been drawn into the Mastermind's twisted web.

"ShadowDancer06" typed, "Anyone have any real info on the Mastermind? Sick of these dead ends."

"Same," replied "LostInTheEchos." "I've been digging for weeks, but it feels like we're chasing shadows."

"Maybe that's how they want us to feel," Emma typed, her fingers hammering against the keys. "Let's compare notes. See if anything lines up."

"Alright, then," LostInTheEchos agreed. "I heard from someone that the Mastermind used to be a psychologist. Specialized in human behavior and manipulation."

"Interesting," ShadowDancer06 chimed in. "I've seen their symbol - that eerie eye - linked to an old research institute. But the place was shut down years ago. Some scandal or something."

"An institute?" Emma's mind raced with possibilities. She had never considered that the Mastermind could be connected to a professional institution. "What else do we have?"

"Rumor has it the Mastermind was betrayed by someone close to them," LostInTheEchos added hesitantly. "Could be part of their motivation."

"Betrayal, huh?" Emma mused, her thoughts churning with the new information. A disgraced psychologist with a penchant for manipulation and a taste for vengeance... It was starting to make sense.

"Keep digging" Emma urged her newfound allies. "Every clue might lead us closer to the truth."

"Be careful" ShadowDancer06 warned. "The more we know, the more dangerous this game becomes."

"Agreed" LostInTheEchos concurred. "But we're all in too deep now. There's no going back."

"Let's do this" Emma was determined, her resolve unwavering. "Together, we can bring the Mastermind down."

As she read their messages of agreement and determination, Emma felt a flicker of hope. Maybe, just maybe, they could beat the Mastermind at their own game.

"Time to connect the dots" Emma whispered, her eyes scanning the forum for more information on the enigmatic figure pulling the strings. She would not rest until the truth was revealed, no matter the cost.

The sound of Emma's fingers tapping on the keyboard filled the room, creating a rhythm that matched the beat of her racing heart. It had been hours since she'd spoken to the other players, and every lead seemed to take her deeper into a maze of shadows and secrets.

"Come on," Emma muttered under her breath, her chestnut hair falling over her face as she leaned closer to the screen, eyes scanning for that one clue that would give her the breakthrough she needed.

"Gotcha," she whispered triumphantly as she stumbled upon a personal blog post with a headline that caught her attention: "The Dark Side of Psychological Research: A Cautionary Tale."

"Someone's bitter" Emma thought as she began to read the post, her deep-set blue eyes locked onto the words. As she delved deeper into the article, it became clear that the author was detailing their experiences at a now-defunct research institute where they claimed to have witnessed unethical practices.

"Is this it?" Emma wondered, her curiosity piqued. She continued reading, her mind racing with possibilities as the blog post outlined a series of experiments designed to test the limits of human manipulation.

"Who would go this far?" she asked herself, unable to shake the feeling that she was getting closer to the heart of the Mastermind's motivations.

"Wait" Emma's breath hitched as she reached the end of the post, her finger hovering over the screen. The author of the blog revealed that they had discovered evidence of a colleague's betrayal – someone who had leaked information about the experiments, leading to the institute's downfall.

"Betrayal" Emma recalled LostInTheEchos' mention of the Mastermind being betrayed by someone close to them. An image formed in her mind – the disgraced psychologist, consumed by vengeance, turning their knowledge of manipulation into a twisted game.

"Is this the Mastermind's origin story?" Emma questioned, her heart pounding in her chest. The sinister nature of the game became more apparent as she pieced together the fragments of information from the blog post and her conversations with the other players.

"Would they really go so far just to prove their control over others?" she contemplated, feeling a chill run down her spine. "How many lives have been ruined by this game?"

"Emma" a voice interrupted her thoughts, causing her to jump. "What are you doing?"

"Nothing" she lied quickly, minimizing the window on her screen. She couldn't risk anyone else getting involved – not when she was so close to uncovering the truth.

"Okay," the voice said, unconvinced. "Just remember, we're here for you."

"Thank you" Emma replied softly, her determination unwavering. She would expose the Mastermind and put an end to the Whispering Game once and for all.

As the door closed behind the departing figure, Emma reopened the blog post, her fingers flying across the keyboard as she copied the information and prepared to share it with her newfound allies. They deserved to know the truth too, and together, they would be unstoppable.

"Time to bring down a monster" Emma murmured, her eyes gleaming with resolve. The game was about to change.

Emma's fingers trembled as she hit 'send,' sharing the vital information with her newfound allies. She knew the risks involved, but the truth mattered more.

"Got to stay focused," she whispered to herself, scanning through an online forum for any more clues.

"Nice try, Emma," a message popped up on the screen, startling her. Her heart raced in her chest. It was a private message from an unknown user.

"Who is this?" she typed back, her pulse quickening with each keystroke.

"Someone who knows what you're up to." The response sent chills down her spine. Was it possible? Had the Mastermind discovered her investigation?

"Leave me alone," she shot back, trying to mask her fear.

"Or what?" came the instant reply, taunting her. "You think you can stop me?"

"Watch me," Emma declared, her determination shining through her trembling hands. She knew the danger she was putting herself in, but she couldn't back down now. There was too much at stake.

"Be careful, dear Emma," the mysterious user warned. "I'd hate for anything...unfortunate...to happen."

"Is that a threat?" she demanded, staring at the screen with wide eyes.

"Consider it a warning," they replied before disappearing, leaving Emma shaken but undeterred.

Chills ran cold down Emma's spine when that last message popped up on the screen, "You wouldn't want to end up like your friend Lucas."

CHAPTER 11

Emma leaned over the table, her deep-set blue eyes scanning the evidence laid out before them. The team had made progress; she could feel it in her bones. Lucas and Detective Thompson buzzed with anticipation as they discussed theories.

"Guys, I think we're onto something," Emma declared, her chestnut hair falling over her shoulder as she straightened up. "We just need to keep going."

"Agreed," Lucas said, his sandy hair sticking up at odd angles, a testament to the hours spent poring over information. "We're close. I can feel it too."

"Good work, kids," Detective Thompson chimed in, his stern expression softening for a moment. "I didn't believe it at first, but you two have really impressed me."

The room felt electric, charged with hope. Emma couldn't help but smile, feeling an unusual sense of camaraderie with this unlikely duo. They were making progress, and she was determined not to let anything stand in their way.

Just as they were about to dive back into their investigation, Detective Thompson's phone rang. His gray eyebrows furrowed as he answered the call. "Thompson here. What do you have for me?"

Emma watched him closely, curiosity gnawing at her insides. But her curiosity slowly morphed into unease as she observed the detective's face grow pale, his hand gripping the phone tightly.

"Are you sure?" he asked, his voice barely audible. "Alright, send me the information. This better be accurate." He hung up and stared at the phone for a moment, seemingly lost in thought.

"Detective?" Emma ventured, her voice cracking slightly. "Is everything okay?"

"Something's come up," he said, avoiding eye contact. "It's about Lucas."

"Me?" Lucas blurted out, his easygoing demeanor suddenly replaced by confusion and fear. "What did I do?"

"An anonymous tip," Detective Thompson muttered, his eyes finally meeting Lucas'. "It seems you're not as innocent as we thought."

"Wait a minute," Emma interjected, her heart pounding. "This has to be a mistake. Lucas is one of the good guys, right?"

"Let's hope so," Detective Thompson murmured, his voice laced with doubt. He glanced at his phone again, his fingers tapping an anxious rhythm on the table. "We'll have to look into this, Lucas."

"Of course," Lucas agreed, his face pale. "I've got nothing to hide."

But as the weight of the accusation hung in the air, a chilling sense of unease settled over the room.

"Detective Thompson, why are there police officers here?" Emma's voice quivered as she eyed the stern-faced men entering the room. She clutched her notebook tightly, her knuckles turning white.

"Emma, I'm sorry," Detective Thompson said, his gaze heavy with regret. "We have to take Lucas in for questioning." The words hung heavily in the air, thick with tension.

"Wait, what?" Confusion and disbelief flooded Emma's face as she turned to Lucas. His sandy hair stuck to his forehead, damp with nervous sweat. "This can't be right."

"Look, Emma," Detective Thompson sighed, running a hand through his cropped gray hair. "I don't want to believe it either, but we've received some solid evidence that suggests Lucas's involvement in a crime."

"Solid evidence?" Emma retorted, her deep-set blue eyes narrowing. "You mean an anonymous tip? How can you be so sure?"

"Emma, please," Lucas pleaded, his voice strained. "Let them do their job. I'll clear this up soon enough."

"Lucas, you don't have to go through this alone," Emma insisted, determination fueling her every word. "We know you're innocent. There must be some mistake."

"Emma, I appreciate your concern," Detective Thompson interjected, his tone firm yet empathetic. "But we need to follow procedure. If Lucas is innocent, he'll be released soon enough."

"Procedure?" Emma spat, her face red with anger. "You're seriously going to put him through this over an anonymous tip? You know as well as I do that the Mastermind could be behind this!"

"Enough!" Detective Thompson barked, his patience wearing thin. He gestured for the officers to approach Lucas. "I'm sorry, but we have no choice. We have to take him in."

"Emma," Lucas whispered, his eyes pleading for understanding. "Please don't give up on me."

"Lucas, I won't," Emma replied fiercely, tears threatening to spill from her eyes. "You can count on that."

As the officers led Lucas away, Emma's chest tightened, a mix of anger and despair clawing at her insides. She knew the Mastermind was testing them, manipulating everyone around them. And in that moment, she vowed to herself – she would not let them win.

"Please don't do this," Emma whispered, choking back tears as she watched the handcuffs wrap tightly around Lucas's wrists. The cold metal seemed to mock the warmth of their friendship, and her heart ached with the injustice of it all.

"Step back, miss," one of the officers commanded, his voice gruff and unsympathetic. Emma obliged, her fists clenched at her sides, ready to fight if necessary.

"Emma, it'll be okay," Lucas reassured her, trying to muster a smile despite the heaviness in his eyes. "I know you believe me."

"Of course I do," she replied fiercely, blinking away tears that blurred her vision. "We're going to get you out of this, Lucas. We won't stop until we do."

"Miss Hartley, give us some space," Detective Thompson said, his words tinged with regret. He glanced at Ava, who stood next to Emma, arms crossed and face a mask of anger and betrayal.

"Detective, how can you just let this happen?" Ava demanded, her voice shaking with raw emotion. "You know Lucas is innocent!"

"Ms. Martinez, I understand your frustration," Detective Thompson replied, avoiding her gaze. His jaw clenched as he added, "But there's nothing more I can do right now."

"Nothing?" Emma echoed, disbelief and fury coursing through her veins. "Lucas is being taken away for something he didn't do, and you're just standing there?"

"Emma," Lucas said softly, catching her eye before the officers guided him toward the exit. "Please, don't let them break us apart. Keep fighting."

A lump formed in Emma's throat as she nodded, unable to speak. She watched helplessly as her friend was led away, each step echoing like a death knell in her ears.

"I'll take you girls to the police station and we can figure this out," Detective Thompson said. As Emma and Ava climbed into the rear seat of the police car they thought, this can't really be happening.

The door to the interrogation room slammed shut, leaving Emma, Ava, and Detective Thompson in a world of cold steel and stark white walls. The echo of Lucas's pleas still hung like a phantom in the air, and Emma's heart pounded in her chest.

"Detective Thompson," she said, her voice trembling with barely suppressed rage, "tell me why you arrested Lucas."

"Emma, it's not that simple—" he began, but she cut him off.

"Tell me!" she demanded, her blue eyes blazing.

Detective Thompson sighed heavily, his gray hair appearing even more lifeless under the harsh fluorescent lights. "We received a tip about evidence connecting Lucas to the crime scene. It seemed credible, so we had to act."

"Who gave you this 'credible' tip?" Ava asked, her arms crossed defiantly.

"An anonymous source," he admitted, his frustration evident. "But the details... They were too specific to ignore."

"Then the Mastermind is playing you!" Emma exclaimed, her hands clenched into fists. "Can't you see it?"

"Look, I'm not happy about this either," he snapped, his stern expression giving way to exasperation. "I don't want to believe that Lucas is involved, but we have to follow the leads we're given."

"Even if those leads are lies?" Emma retorted, her anger undiminished.

Detective Thompson hesitated, his gaze flicking away from her piercing stare. "I don't know, Emma. I just don't know."

"Dang it!" Ava cursed, slamming her fist against the wall. "How can we fight an enemy who's always one step ahead?"

"Maybe we can't," Emma murmured, the weight of hopelessness settling on her shoulders.

"No," Detective Thompson said, a fire suddenly alight in his eyes. "We can't give up. We have to keep fighting, even if it seems impossible."

"Then what do we do now?" Ava asked, her voice barely above a whisper.

"First, we find the truth about Lucas," Emma said firmly, determination stealing her resolve. "And then... Then we bring down the Mastermind, once and for all."

In an angry rage, Emma and Ava left the police station furious about their current situation.

The sun sank below the horizon, casting shadows across the empty street. Emma stared blankly at the spot where Lucas had been arrested, her eyes glazed with unshed tears.

"Emma," Ava said softly, placing a hand on her shoulder. "We need to regroup."

"Regroup?" Emma scoffed, finally tearing her gaze away from the void left by Lucas's absence. "The Mastermind just played us like puppets, Ava. They used Thompson, and now Lucas is paying the price."

Ava sighed, her frustration evident in the tight lines around her eyes. "I know. But wallowing won't get us anywhere."

"Fine." Emma's voice was flat, devoid of emotion. "Let's talk."

"Look, I'm pissed too," Ava admitted. "But we can't let the Mastermind win."

"Win?" Emma's laugh was bitter. "They've already won, haven't they? They manipulated everyone around us, including the police. How are we supposed to fight that kind of power?"

"By not giving up," Ava insisted, her brown eyes fierce. "We keep digging, keep searching. We find proof to clear Lucas's name and expose the Mastermind."

"And then what?" Emma asked, her voice hollow. "What if we're just playing into their hands again?"

"Then we change the game," Ava replied, determination sparking behind her eyes. "We make our own rules and stop reacting to their moves. We take control."

"Is that even possible?" Emma wondered aloud, her gaze drifting back to the fading light in the sky. "Can we really beat someone who knows how to manipulate us so easily?"

"Emma," Ava said, her tone firm. "We have no choice but to try. Lucas is counting on us."

"Lucas..." Emma whispered his name, feeling her resolve harden like steel. She knew Ava was right; they couldn't afford to give up, not when their friend's life was at stake.

"Fine," she agreed, her voice steady despite the turmoil churning within her. "We'll find a way to beat the Mastermind at their own game. We'll clear Lucas's name and bring that manipulative bastard down."

"You're right we will," Ava vowed, her eyes blazing with newfound determination.

As they stood together in the encroaching darkness, Emma couldn't help but wonder if they were walking straight into another trap. But with Lucas's freedom hanging in the balance, they had no other choice. They would forge ahead, even if it meant facing the full wrath of the Mastermind.

The morning sun cast a sickly yellow hue over the small, cluttered room that had become their makeshift headquarters. Emma stared at the piles of documents and photographs scattered across the table, each one a piece of a puzzle they had yet to solve. Ava sat opposite her, head in hands, her fiery red hair falling like a curtain around her face.

"Did we miss something?" Emma asked, her voice barely above a whisper. "How did the Mastermind know about Lucas?"

Ava shook her head, letting out a bitter laugh. "We were so sure we were close, but we played right into their hands."

"Maybe..." Emma hesitated, biting her lip as she considered her next words. "Maybe we should retrace our steps, go back to the beginning. There must be clues we overlooked."

"Or traps waiting for us," Ava countered, her eyes narrowing. "What if every step we take is exactly what the Mastermind wants? What if..."

"Enough!" Emma slammed her fist on the table, making both Ava and herself jump. She took a deep breath, steadying her trembling hands. "We can't afford to second-guess ourselves. We have to clear Lucas's name and expose the Mastermind." She paused, locking eyes with Ava. "No matter what it takes."

"Even if it means risking everything?" Ava questioned, her voice low and intense.

"Whatever it takes," Emma repeated, her determination unwavering.

"Alright," Ava agreed, nodding slowly. "It won't be easy, but we'll find a way."

"Exactly," Emma said, her mind racing with possibilities. "Let's start by revisiting our list of suspects. Maybe there's something we missed."

"Fine, but we should be prepared to dig deeper this time. No stone left unturned, remember?" Ava warned, her gaze flicking between Emma and the documents on the table.

"Agreed," Emma nodded, her heart pounding in her chest. "Let's get to work."

As they delved back into their investigation, each new lead only seemed to tangle the web of deceit and manipulation even further. But with every dead end and false clue, Emma's determination to clear Lucas's name and bring down the Mastermind only grew stronger. And for the first time since Lucas's arrest, she felt a glimmer of hope – however fleeting – that they might just be able to turn the tables on their unseen enemy.

Hours later, Emma found herself standing in the dimly lit parking lot outside Ava's apartment. Detective Thompson leaned against his car, arms crossed, face set in a grim line. Ava's expression mirrored his, her eyes hollow and dark.

"Look," Detective Thompson said gruffly, "I know we're all tired, but we can't let this break us."

"Easy for you to say," Ava snapped, her voice cracking. "You didn't have your best friend arrested because of some twisted game."

"Hey," Emma interjected, putting a hand on Ava's arm. "We're all in this together, remember?"

"Right," Ava said, swallowing hard. Her gaze flicked between Emma and Detective Thompson, her defiance wavering.

"Exactly," Emma agreed, her own voice strained. "We'll clear Lucas's name and expose the Mastermind. But first, we need to regroup and come back at this with fresh eyes."

"Alright," Detective Thompson sighed, rubbing a hand over his stubbled chin. "I'll see what I can do from my end. Keep me posted."

"Will do," Emma said, watching as the detective climbed into his car and drove off into the night. She turned to Ava, who was leaning against the brick wall of her apartment building, shoulders slumped. "Go get some rest, Ava. We'll pick this up tomorrow."

"Emma," Ava began, her voice barely above a whisper. "What if we can't do this? What if the Mastermind is always one step ahead of us?"

"Then we'll find a way to outsmart them," Emma vowed, her chestnut hair whipping around her face as the wind picked up. "We just have to keep pushing forward."

"Okay," Ava said softly, her brown eyes filled with uncertainty. "See you tomorrow."

"Goodnight, Ava," Emma replied, watching as her friend disappeared into the apartment building. She was left alone in the parking lot, the shadows deepening around her.

As she made her way back to her own car, a chill crept down her spine. It felt like someone was watching her. She glanced around nervously but saw nothing amiss. Shaking off the feeling, she fumbled for her keys and unlocked the door.

But before she could climb inside, a single piece of paper fluttered out from beneath the windshield wiper, landing at her feet. Heart pounding, she bent down to pick it up. Scrawled across it in slanted, sinister handwriting were three chilling words:

"Give up now."

Emma's pulse raced, her breath catching in her throat. The Mastermind had been here. Watching. Waiting. And they weren't finished with her yet.

CHAPTER 12

Emma stood before the cracked mirror, her deep-set blue eyes staring back at her, searching for answers. The person she was when this all began felt like a stranger now. She had faced more obstacles than she ever thought possible, but each one had only strengthened her resolve. Fear had given way to determination, and doubt had turned into an unwavering belief in herself.

Emma went downstairs to find Ava in the living room, her curly black hair tied up in a messy bun as she furiously tapped away at her laptop. Her sharp brown eyes flicked between screens, decoding data with unnerving speed.

"Got anything?" Emma asked, trying not to let her impatience show.

"Almost there," Ava said, her fingers never slowing. "Just give me a minute."

As they waited, Detective Thompson entered the room, his cropped gray hair a stark contrast to his stern expression. He had been reluctant to join their cause, but Emma's unwavering passion for the truth had won him over.

"Alright, kids," he grumbled. "What's the plan?"

"First, we need to find the Mastermind's location," Emma said, her mind racing. "Ava's working on that. Then, we'll need to come up with a strategy to confront them."

"Confronting the Mastermind is dangerous," the detective warned. "We have no idea who we're dealing with or what they're capable of."

"Exactly," Emma replied firmly. "That's why we need to stick together and rely on our strengths. Ava's technical skills and your experience, Detective. We can do this."

"You're right, we can," Ava declared, slamming her laptop shut. "I got the location. Time to end this game."

Ava explained, "based upon everything I have researched on the Mastermind, it all leads back to the abandoned warehouse. He's got to be there!"

"Let's go," Emma said, her heart pounding in her chest. She would confront the Mastermind and expose their true identity, no matter the cost. And with her newfound inner strength and the support of her allies, she knew they had a fighting chance.

Emma glanced around at her allies, their faces a mixture of determination and apprehension. She felt the weight of their trust, and with it, the responsibility to bring this dangerous game to an end. "Alright," she said, taking a deep breath. "We can't go in blind. We need to be smart about this."

"Agreed," Detective Thompson nodded. "First, we have to assume that the Mastermind knows we're coming. They've been one step ahead of us this entire time."

"Let's finish this," Detective Thompson growled, adjusting his holstered gun. "For all those who've suffered because of this twisted game."

With their plan set, the trio moved as one, a unified force determined to confront the Mastermind. The sun was beginning to drop below the horizon, casting long shadows across the city streets as they hurried toward their destination.

Emma's pulse quickened with each step. Her thoughts raced and her senses sharpened. This was it. Everything had led to this moment, and she couldn't afford to fail now. The lives of her friends, the players in the game, hung in the balance.

"Stay close," Detective Thompson warned as they approached the warehouse. "We don't know what's waiting for us in there."

"Alright," Emma said, her voice steady despite the fear that clawed at the edges of her mind. "Let's go."

As one, they stepped into the darkness, each determined to face whatever horrors awaited them within. For united, they stood their best chance of ending the Mastermind's reign of terror once and for all.

The warehouse loomed before them, a monolith of decay. Shadows clung to the peeling paint and broken windows, swallowing the remnants of the day's fading light. The wind whispered through the open door, beckoning them inside.

"Stay sharp," Emma murmured as she led her friends into the cavernous space. The air was heavy with disuse and dampness; it clung to their skin like a shroud. She could feel the tension radiating from her companions, their nerves strung taut like the strings on a violin.

"Watch your step," Detective Thompson cautioned, his eyes scanning the shadows for any sign of danger.

"Emma," Ava whispered, her voice unsteady. "Are you sure about this?"

"More than anything," she replied, her determination unwavering. She knew what was at stake, and she refused to let her fear hold her back. "We've come too far to turn back now."

As they ventured deeper into the warehouse, the darkness pressed in around them, threatening to suffocate them in its cold embrace. Their footsteps echoed off the concrete floor; each step felt like a drumbeat heralding their arrival.

"Let's move," Emma commanded, her resolve steeling her against the fear that gnawed at the edges of her mind. They crept forward, their breaths shallow, their hearts pounding in their chests.

"Something doesn't feel right," Detective Thompson muttered, his hand tightening around the grip of his gun.

"Stick to the plan," Emma insisted, her voice steady despite the dread that coiled in her gut. She couldn't afford to let her guard down now. Not when they were so close.

The door at the end of the corridor loomed before them, an ominous barrier to the truth that lay beyond. Emma's fingers curled around the handle, her grip unwavering as she turned it and pushed the door open.

"Welcome," a voice purred from the darkness, sending shivers down their spines. "I've been expecting you."

"Of course you have," Emma shot back, her fear giving way to a burning determination. "But you won't be in control for much longer. We're here to put an end to your twisted game."

"Bold words," the Mastermind replied, their voice dripping with malice. "But I'm afraid you're mistaken."

"Am I?" Emma challenged, her blue eyes blazing with defiance. Her mind raced, searching for the right move, the perfect strategy to unmask their enemy and bring them down. She knew she had to stay one step ahead if they were to survive this final confrontation.

"Enough talk," Emma snapped, her voice cutting through the darkness like a knife. "Show yourself."

"Patience, my dear," the Mastermind taunted, their laughter echoing off the warehouse walls. "All in good time."

"Ava, be ready," Emma whispered, her eyes scanning the shadows for any sign of movement. She could feel her heart pounding against her ribs, but she refused to let fear take hold.

"Your friends won't save you," the Mastermind sneered. "They're just pawns in my game."

"We're not your toys," shouted Emma.

"Ah, but you are," came the reply, cold and merciless. "And I've been pulling the strings all along."

"Stop trying to get into our heads," Ava warned, her voice laced with anger. "It won't work."

"Too late," the Mastermind hissed, their tone mocking. "The game is already won."

"Who is it, Emma?" Ava demanded, her eyes wide with disbelief.

"Someone who's been with us from the beginning," Emma replied, her voice barely above a whisper. She took a deep breath, steeling herself for what she was about to reveal. "It's—"

The warehouse shook with the Mastermind's enraged howl, cutting her off as they scrambled to regain control of the situation.

"Your time is up," Emma declared, resolute and unyielding. "We know who you are. And we're coming for you."

With every step they took, the tension in the warehouse grew thicker, like a suffocating fog. Emma's heart pounded in her chest, adrenaline coursing through her veins. She clenched her fists, gritting her teeth as she prepared for the final showdown.

Detective Thompson walked ahead of Emma and Ava into the dark room.

"Alright," Detective Thompson said, his voice steady but firm. "We've got them cornered. No more games, no more manipulations."

A loud thud noise was heard and Detective Thompson's body fell unconsciously to the ground.

And then, with a suddenness that was both shocking and terrifying, the Mastermind emerged from the shadows, their identity now laid bare for all to see. Gasps escaped from Ava and Emma as recognition dawned on them.

"Impossible," Emma whispered, her eyes wide with disbelief. "Principal Dawson?"

CHAPTER 13

The Mastermind's eyes gleamed with malicious satisfaction, their smirk a cruel mirror of the shock etched across Emma's face. They reveled in her pain and confusion, basking in the chaos they had woven around her.

"Impossible," Emma whispered, her voice trembling with the weight of her disbelief. The sound of her own voice seemed distant, as if she were an observer of this nightmare rather than its focal point. "Why? Why would you do this?"

"Ah, the ever-curious Emma," the Mastermind mused, their tone dripping with disdain. "Always seeking answers, even when they're standing right in front of you."

"Tell me!" Emma demanded, her anger momentarily drowning out the crushing betrayal that threatened to suffocate her. She clenched her fists at her sides, nails biting into her palms. "Give me one good reason!"

"Reason?" the Mastermind echoed, feigning innocence. "I previously worked as a psychologist at an institute and was betrayed by those close to me. Now I work as a principal so I can continue by research on human manipulation."

"I did it because I could, because it was fun to watch you squirm, uttered the Mastermind."

"Fun?" Emma spat, the word tasting bitter on her tongue. "You call ruining lives fun?"

"Indeed," the Mastermind replied, her smile never faltering. "You must admit, it's been quite the game."

"Game?" Emma thought, her mind racing. Every interaction, every shared moment – all just pieces in a twisted game of manipulation and betrayal. "This isn't a game," she whispered, more to herself than to the Mastermind. "This... this is my life. We are not your lab rats!"

"Ah, but life is the ultimate game, dear Emma," the Mastermind responded, seemingly delighted by her anguish. "And I've always played to win."

"Your victory won't last," Emma vowed, the fire of determination flaring within her. "I'll find a way to bring you down, no matter what it takes."

"Bold words," the Mastermind conceded, nodding in mock admiration. "But as I've said before, only time will tell."

"Time," Emma mused, a plan beginning to form amidst the whirlwind of her thoughts. "Yes, time will reveal the truth. And when it does, you'll regret ever crossing me."

"Is that a threat?" the Mastermind asked, their smile never wavering.

"Consider it a promise," Emma replied, her voice resolute despite the tears that threatened to spill from her eyes. "One I intend to keep."

"Enough of this," Emma demanded, her voice trembling with barely contained fury. "Tell me why you did all this. What were you trying to achieve?"

"Isn't it obvious?" the Mastermind replied, their eyes gleaming in the dim light. "My ultimate goal was to frame you and your little friends for crimes you didn't commit."

"Frame us?" Emma gasped, her chestnut hair falling over her eyes as she tried to process the revelation. "But... why?"

"Because I can," the Mastermind answered, their sinister grin widening. "You've all been such fascinating pawns in my grand design. I wanted to see how far I could push you before you broke."

"Push us?" Emma's deep-set blue eyes flashed with anger. "You destroyed our lives!"

"Ah, but that's where you're wrong," the Mastermind countered, a wicked glint in their gaze. "I gave your lives purpose. Without me, you'd be nothing more than ordinary teenagers, bored and lost in this mundane world."

"You're sick," Emma hissed, clenching her fists at her sides.

"Perhaps," the Mastermind conceded, seemingly unfazed by her accusation. "But I prefer to think of myself as an artist, painting with the darkest shades of human nature."

"An artist?" Emma scoffed, her disdain evident. "You're a monster."

"Monster, artist... it's all a matter of perspective," the Mastermind mused, tilting their head in mock contemplation. "But enough philosophizing. Let's return to the matter at hand, shall we? You now know my ultimate goal, and there's nothing left for us to discuss."

"Nothing left to discuss?" Emma repeated incredulously. "You think we'll just let you walk away after everything you've done?"

"Of course not," the Mastermind replied, their confidence unshakable. "But that's the beauty of it all – there's nothing you can do to stop me."

"Emma..." Ava spoke up, her voice barely a whisper. She and Ava stood frozen in disbelief, their faces reflecting a mix of shock and horror.

As Emma and Ava look down at Detective Thompson's unconscious body lying face down on the ground, the

Mastermind laughs, "good luck explaining how you assaulted that detective." A large red bump is visible on the back of the detective's head.

"Emma," Ava whispered, finally breaking her stunned silence. "What do we do now?"

The abandoned warehouse seemed to close in around them.

"First," Emma said through clenched teeth, forcing herself to focus, "we need to get out of here."

"Agreed," Ava muttered, her jaw set with determination as he glanced nervously around the darkened space. "But how do we prove our innocence?"

"Piece by piece," Emma replied, her heart pounding in her chest. "We'll find the evidence to clear our names. We have to."

"Are you sure we can?" Ava asked, her eyes filled with doubt and fear. "They've gone to great lengths to trap us, Emma. What if we can't escape this game?"

As they moved cautiously towards the exit, the weight of their situation seemed to grow heavier with each step. Emma's mind raced, trying to untangle the web of deceit that had ensnared them all. Her friends, once her lifelines, now looked to her for guidance, their trust both a comfort and a burden.

"Emma," Ava said quietly, her voice tinged with uncertainty. "I'm scared."

"Me too," she admitted, grasping his hand tightly. "But we can't let fear control us. They want us to be afraid, to panic. That's how they win."

"Right," Ava chimed in, taking a shaky breath. "We need to stay strong and stick together. No matter what."

"Exactly," Emma agreed, nodding firmly. "We've come this far, and we won't let them destroy us. We're better than that."

As they stepped out of the warehouse, leaving the darkness behind, Emma knew that their lives had been irrevocably changed by the Mastermind's twisted game. But with every ounce of courage she could muster, she vowed to fight back and reclaim their lives.

Emma's heart pounded in her chest, the sound of sirens echoing through the air. She glanced over Ava, her eyes wide with fear.

"Run little rabbits," the Mastermind's voice yelled from the warehouse. "Those sirens are for you!"

They were on the run, the authorities hot on their trail.

CHAPTER 14

"Go!" Emma shouted, adrenaline surging through her veins as she took off down the crowded streets of Crestwood. Her deep-set blue eyes scanned the surroundings, searching for a way out, an escape.

Ava sprinted alongside her, her long legs propelling her forward. "We can't keep this up," she panted, "they're closing in on us."

"Got it!" Emma called back, rounding a corner and weaving through the throngs of people. The sirens grew louder, and she knew that time was running out. She ducked into a narrow alley, her chestnut hair catching briefly on a rusty fire escape before she yanked herself free.

"Think, Emma," she muttered under her breath, her mind racing. "What would Dad do?"

The answer came to her in a flash. Disguise. If they couldn't see her, they couldn't catch her. Emma ripped off her jacket, stuffing it into a nearby dumpster, her fingers trembling with urgency. She sprinted back onto the street, feeling exposed and vulnerable. Every passing stranger could be an informant, every glance a betrayal.

"Hey!" a voice called out from behind her. Emma's heart seized in panic, but she forced herself to keep running, faster and harder than ever before. The sirens grew fainter, but she knew the authorities wouldn't give up so easily. They had left a digital trail, and it was only a matter of time before they were found.

The thunderous roar of helicopter blades sliced through the air above them as they sprinted down yet another unfamiliar street. Emma felt a chill run down her spine; she knew that they were closing in, and with every step she took, the danger seemed to grow.

"Stop right there!" A voice barked behind her, causing Emma to glance over her shoulder, only to see a police officer gaining on her.

"Can't do that, sorry!" she shouted back, forcing herself to put one foot in front of the other, her deep-set blue eyes scanning the area for any possible escape route.

"Left, then right," Ava's voice chimed in, her evasion instincts guiding Emma through the labyrinthine streets of Crestwood. "There's a small courtyard up ahead – lose them there!"

"Thanks, Ava," Emma whispered, gritting her teeth as she followed her friend's directions. The weight of their situation threatened to crush her, but Emma knew she had to stay focused. They had to clear their names, and to do that, they had to escape.

"Right behind you," Emma replied, her legs aching from the relentless sprint. They had managed to confuse their pursuers for now, but it wouldn't be long before they were back on their trail. The thought propelled her forward, unwilling to give up even in the face of insurmountable odds.

"Go, go!" Emma urged Ava. Her heart thundered in her chest, the sound echoing in her ears as she sprinted down an alleyway. She could hardly breathe; each gasp of air felt like inhaling fire. Sweat dripped down her face, blurring her vision. But she couldn't stop. She had to keep going.

"Left here!" shouted Ava, turning into another narrow street.

"Wait," Ava panted, pulling out her phone. "We need to disable our GPS."

"Good call," Emma agreed, her fingers trembling as she followed suit. They couldn't afford to leave a digital trail for the authorities. She knew their every move would be scrutinized and used as evidence against them. It was terrifying how easily technology betrayed them, but there was no time to dwell on that now.

"Okay, let's—" Emma started, but her voice caught in her throat when she spotted a nearby security camera. The sickening realization hit her: their faces were being recorded, and countless others like it littered the city.

"Cameras," she whispered, pointing at the ominous device. "We've been caught on video."

"Dang it," Ava cursed, anxiety flashing in her eyes. "What do we do?"

"Keep going," Emma said firmly. "We can't let that slow us down."

"Right," Ava nodded, swallowing her fear. They had no choice but to press on, even as the net tightened around them. "Just... stay aware. And try to avoid the cameras."

"Got it," Ava replied, determination etched on her face. "Let's go."

They sprinted on, ducking through alleys and side streets. Every so often, Emma would glance back, scanning for any sign of pursuit. Her heart raced, her mind spinning with the knowledge that their digital trail might be their downfall.

"Okay," Emma agreed, bracing herself for another run. She knew their every move was being watched, but they couldn't afford to falter. They had to stay strong, no matter what. "Let's go."

Emma's chestnut hair clung to her sweat-drenched face as they stumbled into the abandoned factory. The stench of rust and decaying wood filled their nostrils, but it was a small price to pay for temporary safety.

"Quick," Ava whispered, tossing Emma an old baseball cap she'd found on the floor. "Put this on."

"Thanks." Emma pulled the cap low over her eyes, attempting to conceal her distinctive blue gaze. She glanced at Lucas, who was busy wiping dirt onto his cheeks to better blend into the shadows.

"Listen," Emma breathed, her voice barely audible. "We need to ditch our clothes. If they see us wearing the same outfits we had on before, we're done for."

"Right." Ava nodded, peeling off her hoodie and kicking off her shoes. She tossed them into the darkness, then reached for a nearby tarp to fashion a makeshift dress. Barefoot and wearing the grubby tarp, Ava resembled a ghost more than the girl they knew.

Emma shed her own sweater, shivering in the cold air as she wrapped herself in a dusty sheet. They looked like escapees from a haunted house rather than teenagers on the run, but it would have to do.

"Stay close," Emma warned, edging towards the factory door. "There could be cops around any corner."

They crept through the dimly lit hallways, their footsteps muffled by the damp floor. Emma felt the weight of their pursuers heavy on her shoulders, aware that each passing second brought them closer to capture.

"Shhh," Ava hissed, pulling Emma back as a flashlight beam cut through the darkness. They held their breath, the fear palpable between them.

"Okay," she thought, her mind racing to keep up with their flight. "We need to find a way out of here, and fast."

"Emma!" Ava's sudden cry jerked her back to reality. A police officer stood before them, his gun drawn and aimed at their makeshift disguises.

"Run!" Emma screamed, the two scattered, taking different paths in a desperate bid to confuse their pursuer.

They had to survive, evade capture, and somehow find a way to clear their names. Failure wasn't an option. "Think, think," Emma muttered, her chestnut hair slick with sweat as she crouched behind a dumpster, her blue eyes scanning the alley for an escape route. Her mind raced, overwhelmed by the pressure and fear of being caught.

"Emma, over here!" Ava waved at her from a narrow passage. She sprinted towards her, their hearts pounding.

"Wait," Ava said, holding up a hand. "I hear footsteps."

"Hide!" Emma hissed, ducking behind a stack of wooden crates. Emma and Ava, breathing shallowly and quietly.

"Emma and Ava!" The voice belonged to Lucas, as he emerged from the shadows, followed by a small group of familiar faces from school. "Thank God, we found you."

"Lucas!" Emma felt a flicker of hope. "We're in trouble. We need a plan."

"Of course," he agreed, his expression serious. "But first, you need to come with us."

"They let me out of jail and I gathered a group of friends to help you and Ava" Lucas stated, his grip tightening on Emma's hand.

"Alright," Emma said hesitantly. "Lead the way."

They followed their supposed allies through a labyrinth of alleys and side streets until they reached a secluded courtyard. Emma scanned the area, her heart sinking as she saw the unmistakable silhouettes of police officers.

"Lucas," she whispered, panic gripping her chest. "What's going on?"

He turned to face her, his eyes cold and betraying no emotion. "I'm sorry, Emma. But we had no choice."

"WHAT?!" Ava roared, shoving Lucas away. "You led us into a trap?!"

"Quiet!" one of the officers barked, stepping forward with his gun drawn. "You're all under arrest."

"Lucas...why?" Emma's voice trembled as she stared at him, betrayal cutting through her like a knife.

"Survival," he replied, shrugging. "We were offered a deal. It was either you or us."

"How could you?" Emma spat, tears streaming down her cheeks as she struggled to hold back her sobs. "We trusted you!"

"Emma, don't," Ava whispered, her hand on Emma's shoulder. "Save your strength. We'll find a way out.

CHAPTER 15

"Hands on your head!" The officer's voice boomed as Emma found herself surrounded by the cacophony of chaos enveloping her. She could barely hear herself think over the shouting and the clicking of handcuffs.

"Get down on the ground!" another officer commanded. Panic surged through Emma's chestnut hair and deep-set blue eyes, widening with fear as they darted from one stern face to another. Her heart pounded in her chest, a relentless drum echoing the turmoil around her. Confusion clouded her thoughts, tangling them into an impenetrable knot.

"Wha-what's happening?" she stammered, her voice barely audible above the din.

"Quiet! You're under arrest!" an officer growled, gripping her arm tightly. Emma blinked back tears, feeling as if the air had been sucked out of her lungs. How did it come to this? She'd only been trying to uncover the truth, but now she was ensnared in a web far more tangled than she'd ever imagined.

"Please tell me what I did wrong," cried Emma.

"You're under arrest for murder and assault of a police officer, Miss Hartley," the officer advised.

Emma's heart sank in her chest as the officer explained.

"We received an anonymous tip that the murder weapon involved in a recent homicide was located within a graveyard nearby," the officer said.

"We found your fingerprints on the knife and the blood on the knife belongs to the victim," stated the officer.

All the hair on Emma's neck stood on end as she remembered picking up the bloody knife and dropping it when she was in the graveyard.

"Please," she whispered, her voice trembling, "I didn't do anything wrong."

"Save it for the judge," the officer holding her arm replied, his face stony and unforgiving.

Emma's thoughts raced, desperately searching for any rationale, any escape from the nightmare that had engulfed her reality. The more she sought, the more apparent it became that she was ensnared, a mere pawn in a bewildering game. The metallic click of handcuffs around her wrists sent a shiver down her spine, signaling an irreversible shift in her world.

"Stand up!" commanded another officer, his icy gaze penetrating Emma. The weight of their stares closed in on her, reminiscent of a pack of wolves encircling their prey.

"Please," she uttered, her voice barely audible. "I don't understand."

"Up!" came the stern and unforgiving order.

Emma's knees quivered as she compelled herself to rise, the handcuffs cutting into her wrists with each motion. The officers loomed over her, their uniforms sharp and imposing, badges reflecting the harsh fluorescent lights.

"Search her," the first officer ordered, and Emma flinched as rough hands explored her, delving into her pockets. They made her feel diminutive, exposed—an intruder ensnared in a labyrinth of darkness and deception.

"Got her phone," announced another officer, holding it aloft like a prize. In sync with the revelation, the device vibrated, its sudden noise rupturing the tense silence that hung over the room.

"Is that...?" Emma hesitated, her eyes fixed on the phone—a slender lifeline amidst the chaos. "Can I...?"

"Quiet!" snapped the officer gripping her arm.

"Let her see it," interjected another, curiosity tinging his tone. The officer with her phone hesitated before thrusting it into Emma's trembling hands.

"Make it quick," he warned.

Emma's heart pounded, her breaths shallow and rapid. Her thumb hovered over the screen, torn between the urgency for answers and the dread of what those answers might unveil.

"Please... tell me what's happening," she implored, her voice catching in her throat.

"Read the message," the curious officer urged, a hint of impatience creeping into his voice.

"Who's it from?" demanded a tall officer, looming over her shoulder like a shadow.

"Unknown," she whispered, her chest tightening with anxiety.

"Read it out loud," he ordered, his tone harsh and unyielding.

As her eyes scanned the words, Emma's heart pounded furiously in her chest. The message was brief, but its meaning cut through her like a dagger:

"The game never ends, Emma. Thanks for playing."

About the Author

Pennsylvania native Aaron Shultz grew up in a small western Pennsylvania town. He has always loved telling scary stories and haunted tales along with exploring local folklore. When he's not thinking of new ways to scare people, he spends most of his time with his wife and kids. With a passion for the outdoors, he and his family can usually be found camping, kayaking, or exploring new outdoor adventures.